A Life's Madcap Journey

By

ALAN NURTHEN

Dedication

To my family and friends who have supported me in my wild ride through life. Thanks for putting up with me!

Acknowledgment

I am a lucky man and I'd like to thank the people at Penguin Book Writer for their work on my book.

Contents

A Life's Madcap Journey
(A wild ride through a life well-lived)

I've been stabbed twice. Well, stabbed once. And slashed once. Both times in the face.

But it didn't mar my looks. It gave them a bit of an edge.

Oh, and I should mention that I stabbed a guy when I was seventeen.

Don't get me wrong. I'm not a thug. I don't have a police record. Not even an outstanding fine.

The stabbing was just a part of life when I grew up in the world of the late 1960s. These were divisive times, and the war in Vietnam added a lot of heat to society.

And that incident of self-protection, when I stabbed a printer's laborer with a Stanley knife as the mob closed in on me for another unauthorized haircut, changed the way apprentices were treated in the printing industry. There would be no more initiations for apprentices, which included stripping them and rubbing printing ink into their genital area or ganging up and cutting our long hair. This was the late sixties when long hair was a badge. It differentiated those with long hair from the "straights."

After the police and the Printing and Kindred Printing

Industries Union investigated the case, there would be no more bullying or harassment of young apprentices.

When my hair was almost cut again by the printers at work and after I stabbed the laborer, half the people wanted to kill me while the rest of the factory was on my side. This made things very difficult for me, so I was transferred to another printing factory in the city. This was good news as they put me on the night shift. That meant I could go surfing every day, go home and get some sleep and then leave for work late in the night.

When my hair was super short after the illegal haircut, I started wearing a paper bag on my head. I cut out eye holes and a hole for my mouth so I could eat. I never wore it at home but would put it on every time I went out. On the drive home from the printing factory soon after the haircut, I was wearing my paper bag when a policeman pulled me over. He wanted to know why I had a paper bag on my head. I removed the bag and pointed to my hair, but the cop didn't get it. He told me to take the bag off my head and not to drive again while wearing it. As soon as he left, I put the bag on my head and drove home. I continued to wear the paper bag until my hair grew back to an acceptable length.

To digress, I want to make it to 95 years of age, at the very least. My Uncle Ron lived to 95, and my Auntie Joy too. But my Auntie Bell broke the record and made it to 105! She didn't have dementia and still had all her marbles.

At Bell's 100th birthday in 2013, when my wife Vera asked if she could take a photo of Bell holding the Queen's letter, Bell said, "Stuff the Queen, where's Julia Gillard's letter?"

Good old Bell, a labor voter and a staunch Republican to the last.

Aunty Bell was the wife of Bob Longton, a sheep farmer. A tough old bird, Bell was responsible for all of the household duties on the farm, including the feeding of the rough-as-guts shearers. Uncle Bob looked after the sheep, and took out any wandering dingo's when they tried to attack the large flock.

On the cover of one of the numerous paperback versions of "Kokoda," the one published in 2004 - the book by master Australian history writer Peter Fitzsimons - Uncle Bob is on the right of the photo with a typical rolly hanging from his mouth. Bob was part of the AIF who took over from the "chocolate" soldiers defending Australia in New Guinea. The choco soldiers were basically untrained in fighting and were the support backbone of the army – cooks, paper pushers etc., who nonetheless put up a brave fight against the Japanese and held the territory until the AIF were sent in to replace them.

Aunty Bell married Bob after the end of the Second World War, and when I asked her how Bob had managed in New Guinea, she said: 'Knowing Bob, he probably enjoyed it.' That was Uncle Bob. He could be as mad as a hatter.

A Baby

When I was a baby, around seven months old, my Dad, when digging a drain for the laundry he was finishing at the house, left me with Trixie, the dog he'd just bought home.

'A dog for the baby to grow up with', Dad said.

Mum wasn't impressed, saying: 'We've already got 3 mouths to feed; now we have a dog to feed as well?'

But without that dog, Trixie, I wouldn't have made my first year of life.

With my Mum, Mona.

Dad went upstairs to the back of the house to make a cup of

tea, leaving Trixie with me. Not long after Dad got there, the dog started going off, reacting big time. Dad ran downstairs and found a brown snake slithering from a hole in the newly dug trench, trying to crawl up into the pram. This was one of those prams from the time when I was up high in a cradle type of thing, and the snake was slithering up the metal support legs. Good old Trixie kept the snake occupied till Dad got there. Dad picked up a shovel and killed the deadly reptile.

When Mum heard what happened, she happily welcomed the dog to the family.

Good old Trixie.

Then everything changed when I was 7 years old.

I had a life-changing experience in the playground at Hornsby Primary School, where I had this strange feeling of being in another zone. Like I was outside of everything, looking in.

The milkman used to drop a few cartons of fresh milk in the playground every day, and on one such day, I gulped down my milk, which was always warm sitting in the sun while the kids were still in class … and then, suddenly, I had this life-changing experience!

I felt stoned but didn't realize what the feeling was until many years later when I first smoked a joint. This strange, intense feeling was telling me that there was a different way of living life.

My insight gave me a different way of doing things. Money was never an issue for me, but finding the right path in life, a path that would let me earn enough to live and do my own thing. Greed was never an issue; a productive life was what I was searching for ... And I made one.

Do your own thing and believe in what you are doing. As Richard Branson stated, along the lines of ... 'If you have a business that supports you, and you love what you do for a living, then you have a successful business.' The greed of money was never mentioned, but the quality of life was.

As a young boy, as early as I can remember, I started to fall in love with music. I loved the sound and the rhythm. My older cousins were into Elvis and the fifties bands, and I came in later with the sixties music. The music really inspired me! I grew up in an era when music was probably as good as it ever gets. From 1962 to the early-Seventies. I'm blessed to have come of age in that period of time.

But I also believe in all the peace, love and goodwill that came alive in the mid-1960s. I've carried the belief all this way. What happened back then has shaped my life.

Childhood

When I was around 8 or so, my favorite game was playing bomber pilots using the headphones and other gear that my Dad brought home from the Second World War as a member of the Australian Air Force.

If any of the local girls were involved then we changed the game to airline pilots and stewardesses.

Girls weren't flying planes in those days.

There were plenty of kids in the neighborhood, all with different ideas, so it was never a problem working out what games to play.

Along with bomber pilots, our favorite activity was playing in the vast bush behind our houses in Silvia Street, Hornsby. We used to roam the bush every day after school and on the weekends, playing whatever games we came up with. Playing hide-and-seek was a great game as there were so many places to hide in the bush. When we were not playing hide-and-seek, then we'd play in the street. Touch football was a fun game because it involved every one of both sexes. So did cricket.

When I was about 10 years old, we made a wooden fort behind our house. It was Dad's land down there - which at one time was a tennis court for Mum. Dad had now used the land for the storage of wooden banana crates and the hessian bags that covered the bananas. The land down there was big with areas of clay dirt and wild bush. Once the fort was made at the bottom of the pathway from Dad's place, which took up half the day, we proceeded to grab old plumbing pipes, stuff one end with clay, drop a penny bunger down the tube, drop in marble on top; aim it and fire!

It was great fun and we were having the time of our lives. Then, the local parents heard the noise of the marbles zinging off the wooden boxes and went to investigate.

They freaked!

We had to dismantle the fort, and the parents took our left-over firecrackers.

These were the days when we used to celebrate Guy Fawkes Day.

Everyone, including our parents, had their own stash of fireworks. On Guy Fawkes Day, we had a big party down the back of Dad's house - with a huge bonfire raging and everyone having the time of their lives.

But with the penny bungers and the fort, we didn't think of the worst outcome. We didn't think of someone losing an eye. Or someone dead. We were just kids with no conception of the word "death."

We thought it was great fun.

Around this time, my sister Sue and I were playing next door in Mr. Curtis's house. We were way down his backyard, which dropped off quite a way where it descended.

Sue picked up a stick – which turned out to be a baby brown snake! It tried to bite her, so she bashed it to death against a rock. We hung it up by the head with a piece of string and threw rocks at it until it fell apart.

Another time, Mr. Curtis was walking deep in his backyard at night when he fell into a meter-deep trench. We had dug the trench to play war games.

Like I said, we were just kids with an endless search for whatever we could get away with.

The bush behind our house was thick back then, but it's almost built out now. When I was a baby and Dad was finishing the house, Mum went to put the washing on the backyard clothesline when she saw a crocodile! She rushed inside to tell Dad, but Dad assured her that we were "too far south to have crocodiles." Dad checked it out and found a large tree goanna with a long neck and sharp claws prowling about in the yard.

Dad went down and shooed it away, and Mum was reasonably safe to finish the washing.

One of the things I liked to do as a kid was a solo event. I'd lay in the backyard of the house and just stare at the clouds. I first became aware of the importance of light and how you could see the cloud formations change before your eyes.

I was seven years old over the Christmas holidays in 1956. At Christmas, one of Dad's presents to me was a small handyman's tool kit. This wasn't plastic, like today. It was the real thing. A mini-saw with a steel blade.

Over the six-week summer holidays - which seemed like years for a seven-year-old - I was itching to cut something - other than *more* wood. I was prowling around the yard, searching for something to cut. Then I spotted the rubber tree. Dad told me to stay away from it. I had to make two important decisions. To stay away from it. Or, you know, cut it a little bit. I started to cut off rubber stems. Then Dad saw me. Being a sprightly seven-year-old, I figured I could outrun him. He gave chase, and I bolted.

He chased me around three-quarters of the yard and then caught me – just short of the rubber tree. Well, that was it. I was dragged inside by my shirt collar, and Dad told Mum what I did. He then took off his leather belt and gave me a few good whacks around the bum. Okay, Dad. Thanks - lesson learned.

I guess I was lucky. Very lucky. I had a perfect childhood with attentive, loving parents. My father, Walter (Wal), and mother,

Mona, along with my cousins and all the other kids who lived in the neighborhood to play with.

My parents welcomed everyone unlike most Anglo-Australians who had resentment for the immigrants from Europe and Asia. Mum and Dad respected everyone as equals and treated everyone with the respect they deserved. Mum and Dad were loved by my friends as easygoing people with "no hangups."

With Mum and Dad. "Whose running this country anyway!"

In 1970, I completed my Lithographic Printing apprenticeship 12 months earlier than I expected due to the fact that the law had changed and apprenticeships were now reduced from five years of servitude to four. This early "get out of jail free card" was a blessing for my ambitions and I immediately booked a passage on the first P&O ship that was available.

In April of 1971, aged twenty one, I was sailing to South Africa to chase my dream waves, courtesy of the stoke instilled in me at thirteen years of age via Bruce Brown's film, *The Endless Summer.*

Returning to Africa for the third time in 1975, some of my professional surfer friends and acquaintances I hung out with at the beach were against Apartheid. Can't blame them.

But demonstrating against Apartheid outside of South Africa, in my mind, wasn't very effective and would have no bearing or effect on the Apartheid regime. In my mind, the truly effective way to see it firsthand and to become involved with the people – both black, brown and white - was inside the country, where I could spread my ideas of equality through both talk and action. I also found it extremely hypocritical of the Australian government to criticize Apartheid when their treatment of our own indigenous people was so shocking.

On my first surfing trip to South Africa in 1971, I was appalled at how society was split down the middle according to race. In fact, after only five months in the country, I was so angry at the South African government and the absolute control they had – with the brutal power to back it up - that I couldn't wait to fly out to Europe and commence the second leg of my trip. What I saw over those five months politicized me for the first time in my young life. It became a way for me to show the oppressed colored people that not all white people saw them as slaves or second-class citizens.

When I returned to South Africa in 1972, I extended my network of friends from all races and backgrounds and believed that I was at least having a small but significant effect on the people I met.

I really believed that I was achieving something positive through my actions and that I was flying well under the radar. However, later that year, when I rode my trail bike from the farm out back of Durban, where I was living to the beachfront to collect my surfboard from the flat of some fellow Aussie friends and hit the waves, little did I know that I was walking into a shit storm.

As I waxed my board in the front room, nine stories up, and scanned Durban's beach breaks for the best waves, I heard a loud and authoritative knocking on the front door of the flat. The African housemaid, "Aunty," answered the door to reveal two huge Afrikaans detectives and then retreated to the kitchen area. The two white cops immediately spotted the Durban Poison piled up like the pyramid of Cheops on the dining room table - with my Aussie mates hoovering the weed through their clay chillum pipes.

The two detectives then told everyone in the room that this was their third warning and that they were to hand over their passports as they would now be deported back to Australia on the next available ship.

Meanwhile, I'm still in the front sun room waiting for my chance to exit through the front door at the first available opportunity. When things calmed down a little, I made my move, strolling through the living room, surfboard under my arm like I was the Urban Spaceman baby: Yeah, I don't exist.

I made it just short of the door when a meaty hand clasped me on the shoulder. The huge Dutch cop told me that they hadn't forgotten about me. They wanted my passport as well.

At this moment, Aunty ran from the kitchen, threw her arms around me and protested loudly and passionately: 'He's a good boy! He's a good boy. He doesn't smoke the dagga. He doesn't smoke the dagga!' The cops peeled Aunty off me and then said they were deporting me too, but not for smoking weed. When I asked them the reason, they said it was because 'I was a bad influence on South African youth. I had too many black friends.'

Such is life in South Africa under Apartheid.

Aunty was brave enough to front up to two Dutch detectives

In 1971, I began making my own surfboards, using the brand name Gypsy Surfboards.

When I was shaping a board I'd rough-shape them in the backyard, and then take them under the house to Dad's workshop and finish the shaping. I was in the habit of throwing out the foam dust and small pieces of cut-off foam. Dad warned me about it. He told me not to throw out the off-cuts because Mum ran the risk of falling over if she tripped on something.

Typical of me - the smart arse who knows everything.

So I continued to throw out off-cuts, and sure enough, Mum tripped over the rubbish and sprained her ankle. I was 22 years old by now, so the leather belt was well in the past - but boy, did I get a talking too! At those times, I'd have to say that I was a typical young surfer, believing that I knew everything ... *Yeah, right.*

If I saw someone for the first time, I'd say: 'Hey man!' My usual greeting.

At home, I disliked doing any of the housework. I'd sometimes put away the dishes when they were washed. I wasn't into mowing the lawns. You know, a spoiled young man. But hey, at that age, all I was thinking of was traveling again. Go and see more of the world! Which I did when I went overseas again in late 1972.

While I was working under the house making boards, I'd put the one I was shaping into the two surfboard-holding racks that Dad built. They were perfect for glassing and for finishing aboard. It was a good set-up down there. Dad worked it out perfectly. He even made a surfboard storage rack. The rack was lined with three-ply, and you could slide 2 or 3 boards onto the wooden rack. Dad designed it at eye- level so you could clearly see what you were doing. Other than Dad's workshop, the rest of the floor under the house was brown dirt. The house was built on a sloping block of land. The front entrance to our house was on one level, but from there on down, it sloped into two stories. Under the house, it was all brown dirt, except for Dad's workshop, where Dad had laid the floor out flat with a spade and then laid concrete onto the floor. His workbench was up against the wall that Dad built for the flat downstairs. To get to the flat, you'd leave Dad's workshop, take a step or two downhill and then go down a set of two or three stairs to the front door of the flat.

Dad had built toilets upstairs for us and one directly below for the flat. To get from our place to downstairs, there was a set of back stairs that ran along the back wall of the house, then turned right where there was a landing which you could jump off into the yard – a big thrill for a 5-year-old preparing for a jump of two meters - then right again to take the final set of stairs down to the backyard.

The perfect setup for a house built on that sloping land, which ran all the way down to the creek at the bottom of the valley.

The back of the house with the stairs, the flat, the sunroom, and my bedroom windows

A well-thought-out house - Dad had a lot of talents, that's for sure.

Then, in 1974, I began working for some of the legends in the surfboard industry: first at Henri Surfboards and then later at Midget Farrelly's Surf blanks. I worked as a front-of-house manager.

In 1974, with a couple of friends, I attended an event at the Town Hall in Sydney for a speaking tour by legendary Gonzo writer Hunter S. Thompson - the author of the book *Fear and Loathing in Las Vegas* - the funniest book I've read. The book was illustrated by Ralph Steadman. His zany cartoons really added to the story. The Town Hall was packed solid. A lot of people wanted to hear what he had to say.

At one time during Hunter's talk, a group of people dressed in shrouds approached the stage. One of them handed up a 4-pound World War 2 bomb. Hunter studied the bomb and then dropped it from the stage to the floor beside the shrouded men's feet. A big sigh of *phew!* Erupted from the audience when the bomb didn't explode.

You couldn't predict what the Gonzo journalist would do next. Hunter S. Thompson freaked out Don Lane at the time when on his TV show, Hunter had his leather jacket over his shoulder – and when he noticed it from the corner of his eye, he shook it off, jumped back and yelled: 'What the fuck's *that!*' It freaked Don Lane out. The show was live - so they had to live with it.

Around this time, in late 1974, I joined the Peninsula Surf Club. It was a surfboard riding club located in Palm Beach, Sydney. I joined the club for the surfing contests and the girls. Some of the members were from St Ives and areas like that. And they had good parties with lots of women in attendance.

Some members of the surfing club were mad rugby league players and played many games away from home. But I was in the club for the surfing only.

The surfboard club hung around the changing sheds on the beach. There were good lefts and rights in front of the sheds, and that's why everyone hung out there.

At the contests the usual winner was Greg Short (my taxi owner friend of the 1980's.) Greg was a powerful surfer and hard to beat if he was in your heat.

Some of the local members, like Mark Short (the Rat, as he was known), had this curious habit of picking up girls. He'd spot a girl walking in the street near the change sheds and yell out: 'Wanna go up to the sand hills and rub wee's?' His response was always the same, and the reaction was always the same.

I don't know if he ever picked up anyone because when there was no surf, he'd be at home nearby watching a TV show. He was on the dole, so it wasn't a problem.

There was quite a gang of surfers at the sheds, including three brothers from The Hideaway at Palm Beach - a huge house rented by their mother, Bev, which was once a hotel and then a hospital. Many of us occasionally stayed at The Hideaway. It was supposed to be haunted and there was a weird vibe about the place. The three brothers from the house were all members of the club. Owen, Lofty and Bod were good surfers, but Owen really stood out. He died a few years ago from brain cancer. A terrible loss. If you also drew Owen in your heat, you wouldn't be impressed. There were some good surfers in the club. People like J.C (John Donnelly) died quite a few years ago now. He had lung cancer. But the saddest thing was, he said to the doctors, 'He couldn't have lung cancer because he gave up smoking nine months ago.'

The club has lost a lot of members over the years: Trevor Arnott; Snake (Paul Roman); Colin Hawkes, who was featured in the early Midget Farrelly skateboard magazine ads; Ross Bailey, a close friend of mine; Dave Wiley … all and more, are now gone.

Trevor Arnott had a house on the way up the hill from Mona Vale on the west side of the road in Ingleside. It burned down during the late 1979 bushfires. I can't remember whether he rebuilt the house or moved. He died a few years ago now. I can't remember how he died. That's my memory for you.

There was a 50th Peninsula Surf Club reunion in November

2017. The party was celebrating the start of the club in 1968. The party was an unusual evening. Most of the guys looked pretty much the same, but some had aged poorly. A member of the club, who M.C.'d the presentation, was constantly interrupted by Andrew Hunter. There's a fool at every party. Hunter made an idiot of himself, and I believe this is what forced him to finally confront his alcoholism. He was so drunk and obnoxious that he'll never forget what he did that night. He ended up catching the bus back to Dee Why, where he lived. Vera was glad to see him go. She never liked him, and for good reason. Once he gave us some paint when we were living at Taiyul Road in North Narrabeen. It was to finish touching up the walls. The paint was useless. Full of globs of white paint. You couldn't ever strain it; it was so bad. Then Hunter rang asking for the paint back. I told him it was useless, and then he went off at me, abusing me and running down my lifestyle. Vera, listening in the background was appalled and said if she ever saw him again, he'll regret it. Hunter had insulted me, and Vera wouldn't have it.

When Hunter finally came around to the house, he rang first to make sure Vera was not at home.

Ha ha. He was actually scared of her. And for good reason, too!

Back to the Surfing Industry. Both of the jobs I had in the industry gave me enough money to live on; and lots of benefits.

At Henri Surfboards I came up with the idea that I could make trips up the north coast every few weeks with a station wagon full of new surfboards, both stored in the back of the car and on the roof.

Good job, as it allowed me one to two days of delivering surfboards to retail outlets from Gosford to Coffs Harbour, leaving a couple of days left over to go surfing at some of my favorite north coast surf breaks. On these trips up the coast before I married Tereza, I always traveled with a good friend Kathy Guildford from St Ives, who used to hang out with the Peninsula Surf Club crew. We'd throw Kathy's self-inflatable surf mat on the top of the surfboards I was delivering. Kathy was great fun and we always had a ball on these trips and then go surfing together when the job was completed.

But at Surfblanks, I worked full-time in the front office and the showroom. It was an honor working for Midget. He was a legend.

Midget didn't like drugs. They would have hampered his achievements. Midget didn't drink much alcohol either. No one used drugs at Surf Blanks when I was there. We were all straight anyway.

A slightly different story at Henri Surfboards. Some of the factory workers smoked a little weed. Chris Henri, myself and my friends didn't smoke the herb.

One Christmas at Surf Blanks in 1976, a surfboard designer from Nirvana Surfboards on the Central Coast shook my hand and deposited a gram of hashish into my palm. He whispered: 'Merry Christmas' into my ear. I kept my hand closed, then later put the hash in my pocket. Midget didn't notice anything.

Tereza had a good Christmas that year!

When I flew back to South Africa in 1975 for three months (nobody hassled me when I returned), I married my long-time South African girlfriend, Tereza James. Then we moved back to Australia. Brennan was born on 26 April 1973 after I was deported from the country in November 1972 "for having too many black friends."

Tereza and I settled in for a short stay at my parents' house. Then we rented a classic house at North Narrabeen, with just the camping ground behind the house, a lake to paddle down or drift down with an outgoing tide before reaching the legendary waves at North Narrabeen.

The house we rented was once the holiday home of Bob and Dolly Dyer - the legendary radio and television hosts of the *Pick a Box* program.

From mid-1975 to mid-1979, that house saw many things change in my life.

The first was in 1977, when Tereza decided that she wanted

to return home to South Africa. She missed her parents and her relatives and friends. That was a major hiccup in my life, and it took me a while to get over it. But even today, Tereza and I remain good friends, strengthened by my two visits in the mid-1990s and then later in 2004-2005 and 2006-2007, when I stayed with my wife Vera at Brennan's home along with his family, wife Sarah and two of my grandchildren, Cade and Alexa.

Tereza has never been out of South Africa except for the trip with me to Australia in 1975. She came out again in 2024 and stayed with Brennan and his family.

In my trips to see Brennan and his family in the 2000s, Vera and I occasionally asked him to think about making a move to Australia.

And then, in 2019 Brennan and his family moved here. Brennan already had an Australian passport because I was his father, as well as a South African passport.

A beautiful country, South Africa, has now been ruined by the ANC government. South Africa was a great country when Mandela became prime minister, but once he retired, the country has gone downhill ever since. Corruption and mismanagement in government, significant unemployment, violent crime, insufficient infrastructure, and poor government service delivery to impoverished communities have added to the problems facing the country.

The next major change in my life was when Tereza, now back in South Africa, asked me to help her by raising some extra money to help raise Brennan. She was now living back at her parents' house, the cheapest alternative for a single Mum. So, we set up an import marijuana scheme. If I was going out on a limb here, then I wanted to be fully protected with a great covering story. So I worked it out with Tereza - I asked her to tell her friends to write to a surfer friend of mine 'who lived at the house for a while but was now surfing somewhere in New Zealand,' asking me to look after his mail. The surfer mentioned never existed, and after the mail built up at home for a while, Tereza posted the first box of weed addressed to the non-existent surfer. The small boxes (containing 600 Durban Poison sticks, roughly the length of my little finger but thinner) were addressed to my non-existent friend. This happened about six times over 18 months before it was discovered by customs.

Whenever a parcel arrived, I made it clear to everyone at the house that the box would sit on the fridge for a week, along with the other mail to my "friend". This worked a treat until a message from the post office was left between the front door and the screen door (behind the 3 plywood covering the door from the bottom to halfway up the door.) The perfect hiding place (unless someone opened the screen door) where the boxes were normally left by the postman.

The classic house at North Narrabeen, 1975

The hiding hole between the screen door and the front door

It tipped me off immediately that the box had been discovered. It was pretty obvious it was busted, for the old woman who worked at the post office nearly choked when I gave her the card to pick up the box. That woman hated me. I was a long-haired, scruffy-looking surfie type. It was now up to our plan.

I went to Woolworths and then back to the car. I was about to pull out when I remembered the postal card. I thought I was probably being watched, so I picked up the box from the post office, and when I got home, I placed it on the fridge with the other mail for my surfing friend. Not 15 minutes after returning home, there was a knock at the front door, and three AFP police officers were standing there. Two men and a woman. A few of my friends were already in the house with my housemate Dean, just sitting around playing guitars and having a good time, so I asked them to leave, with just me, my girlfriend Christine and Dean in attendance. The AFP believed that we would have been into the box and getting high but were perplexed when I told them it was on the fridge with the other mail for my 'friend'. This knocked them back a bit. They asked me if I'd ever been to South Africa, and I said yes three times.

I told them I had mail addressed to me from Tereza and an old friend Tom Thompson, which they read.

They then had me enter the main bedroom with one of the AFP men, with Christine being taken into the second bedroom by the AFP woman. Then, the woman came into the main bedroom with me and one of the men spoke to Chris in the spare bedroom and questioned her again. The two cops got together and found that our stories matched perfectly. Our story, which was well rehearsed, convinced them that we had nothing to do with the drugs. They searched the house and found no incriminating evidence other than a few small containers of seedling weed stashed up near the overhead windows in the kitchen. *Thanks, Dean!* I told him to get rid of the plants as there was a box coming, which in Dean's stupidity, he ignored! When the AFP asked who owned the weed, I gave Dean a filthy look and said they were mine. The cops weren't stupid; they were after an importing charge, and the weed meant nothing to them. They told Christine to flush the tiny little plants in the toilet, which she did.

We then made cups of tea and supplied a plate of biscuits for the AFP. We had a good old natter about nothing in particular. After they finished their tea and the biscuits, they left. And then, a few minutes later, they returned. They forgot to take the box!

I told them to leave it if they liked it, and they had a laugh.

Home and hosed!

We'd fooled the AFP, who took our story hook, line and sinker. That saved me from a 20-year stretch in gaol! In a certain way, I was telling the truth because I didn't even smoke dope then, and all the money I made from selling the weed to friends went straight back to Tereza - other than a few sticks that Christine stashed away. I've never been a big fan of drugs or alcohol, and I believe the AFP police picked up on that.

But my mother, being psychic, had for-seen the outcome in a dream a couple of weeks before the above incident, where she saw cops come to my home. That dream Mum had also helped me to prepare for what was about to happen.

But then, a few years later, when we were packing up our things to store at Mum and Dad's before our trip to America in 1979, I found a Durban poison stick stuck between two saucepans. Then, I found two more sticks stuffed between plastic picnic cups. I couldn't believe it! Chris had this habit of putting things away somewhere - and then forgetting where she put it. If the AFP had searched the house really well - I'd be *caught.* Red-handed with the evidence! A sobering thought indeed.

Speaking of our housemate, Dean reminded me of when I went to Noosa for a holiday in 1978. We were all surfing at a back beach when we noticed a group of large sharks feeding on a school of fish. They were a long way offshore, but then, all of a sudden, we were being buzzed by smaller sharks who were zipping about beneath us. We all headed for shore, but Dean just kept on surfing. We tried to call him to the beach, but he ignored us. When he did finally come in, I asked why he kept on surfing, and he said he was on the same wavelength as the sharks, and they didn't bother him. The fact that Dean was living on magic mushrooms for breakfast, lunch and dinner probably explained his decision!

Speaking of sharks. When I was surfing Sawtell Island in 1970 with my friend Clyde Cameron, we had a run-in with a Tiger shark. Sawtell is the first beach in Coffs Harbour when heading north. I was paddling back out after a good, winding right-hander when suddenly Clyde called out, 'Shark! Shark!'

He paddled for the beach, yelling out. I thought he was kidding me. I paddled up the face of the oncoming wave when I saw under the wave a 5-foot Tiger shark heading straight for me. I pushed my face and body into my surfboard so if the shark hit me I might avoid being knocked out and would stay on my board. I went over the top of the wave and looked around in a panic. The shark had disappeared. I spun around and headed for the beach. I was paddling like a demon, and I overtook Clyde and made it to the beach before him! My board was 6 foot two in length, and I believe the shark, being smaller, thought something was attacking him and took off.

Buster

In 1976, while living in the house at 47 Collins Street North Narrabeen with Tereza and Brennan, I noticed in the local paper there was a family in Newport who was moving overseas and was looking for someone to take their 18-month-old dog, Buster. I responded immediately and went and picked the dog up. I took him to the vet to make sure everything was all right and the vet was amazed that Buster had seven different breeds of dogs in him. He was made up of a cattle dog, an Alsatian, a beagle, a kangaroo dog, a kelpie, a border collie and a greyhound. Wow, what a mix!

At first, I thought that Buster couldn't jump very high, and then I was amazed when I heard the high wooden door to the garage vibrate. Buster had jumped over the garage door with the low roof overhead and made it into the front yard of the house.

Buster had this habit he'd pull on people when they visited. He'd lie on a bean bag, gain their attention and then go down and suck himself off. It blew people's minds! A visitor would say to me what they'd just seen, and I'd reply that it was one of Buster's favorite tricks. He loved freaking people out and did it whenever friends visited the house.

Buster and his natural black-eye liner, "rock 'n roll baby"

Buster and his "question mark" tail

One winter, I drove up to Crescent Head with surfing buddies Clyde Cameron and Peter Banks. On our way back home, I pulled into the small garage at Crescent Head to fill up the car. Without me noticing, Buster jumped out while I was dealing with the car. I paid for the fuel, and we headed home. We drove all the way to the Pacific Highway, 17 kilometers from Crescent Head. I turned around and noticed that Buster wasn't in the back of the station wagon, lying on our surfboards. I freaked! Shit! I left him behind! I turned around and drove all the way back to Crescent Head, panicking all the way - and there he was, sitting next to the petrol pump in the garage. He was looking at every car that passed heading west, so I pulled up opposite the garage, called his name, and he bounded across the road, jumped into the rear of the station wagon and just sat there looking relieved and very embarrassed.

Buster's a faithful dog; He must have known deep down inside that we'd be back for him. He was a great-looking dog, with black eyeliner around each eye and a question-mark tail.

Buster could fight, though. He got into a fight with a bull terrier in the front yard of our house, and the fight was so vicious that I had to jump on their heads to separate them. Buster lost an eye tooth in that fight when he bit the other dog's studded collar.

Buster also had this trick he pulled on the people staying in the camping ground behind the house.

I'd wander over to the beach for a surf, and I'd discover Buster sitting outside a caravan, looking hungry and rejected. The owner of the caravan would take pity on him and give him cooked sausages or meat. Every time I saw Buster bludging from the campers, I'd call out to him. He just ignored it and pretended he never knew me. I always got a laugh from his antics.

Another time when I was heading to the beach for a surf with Buster tagging along, I noticed the dog catcher's van with the cage at the back of the truck full of dogs. I put my surfboard on the ground and opened the cage door. The dogs scrambled out of the cage and took off - hopefully for the safety of home.

When the dog catcher caught sight of what I was doing, he was not impressed - to say the least. He said to me: 'You're the one who should be in the cage. You're nothing but an animal!'

The dog catcher was a tricky old bastard. He'd catch any dogs walking around by using a lure. He'd offer them a few biscuits or something else to eat and then chain them while they were eating. He'd put the dogs in the back of the van, then drive away searching for more victims.

I never had any time for the dog catcher.

But I have to say, Buster was the best dog I ever owned, and he was with me for six wonderful years before he died - from a bloody cattle tick! Nasty little things, cattle ticks.

There was also a bad flood in Narrabeen on Black Friday, the 4th of March 1977. There was so much rain that the river overflowed. Brennan came into Tereza and my bedroom and said that his toys were floating across the floor of his bedroom. Our bedroom was up a step from the lounge room and from Brennan's room, so our room wasn't flooded like the rest of the house. I went out into the backyard with Brennan in my arms, and the Chinese chickens that Dad gave us were all hanging on the wire of their cage to escape the flood waters.

Our flooded back yard, 1977

4th of March, 1977

There was nothing we could do, so we packed up the car and headed up the coast to Coffs Harbour to go surfing for two weeks. When we got back home the waters had receded. We vacuumed the dirt left on the carpet from the flood, and there was no smell because it was salt water that flooded the house and not freshwater, thank goodness.

Fooling the police (again!)

All my life, I haven't put any stock in authority.

The law can be an ass.

With my moral codes and beliefs, I'd have to say I've broken the law occasionally, either through necessity or for purely merciless reasons. I believe that if a law is unjust, then it is your patriotic duty to break it. And the more people who break regressive Machiavellian laws, the sooner those laws will be repealed.

My wife Vera, my step kids Ksenia and Victor and I were living in a large house at 90 Taiyul Road, North Narrabeen. There was a loud knock on the front door. I had just woken up and answered the door to see a bunch of Drug Squad detectives with a warrant to search the house.

Apparently, there was an undercover police officer watching the house who noticed there were a lot of people visiting the property and suspected that Victor was selling drugs. But as it happened, the visitors were friends of the four of us. But the people in the flat downstairs *were* selling drugs.

The detectives who turned up at our place proved to be poorly trained and under-brained and they ran an unsuccessful operation which came up with nothing of any substance.

There was an older cop with them in a full uniform who

became quite aggressive with my family during his questioning, and I let him know in no uncertain terms that if he was going to abuse us, then he could take his warrant and leave the house. In no uncertain terms, I told him that I was not intimidated by his uniform or by him and told him that as far as I was concerned, he was nothing but 'a muppet in fancy dress.' That comment stunned him. He didn't know how to take it, so he calmed down a little. Then, when I noticed that one of them was recording the interview with a camera, I let them know we would require a copy of the tape. The man recording said it was police evidence and we wouldn't have access to the tape. Then, I instructed them to line up while I took down their names and details. The ten detectives did this like a bunch of naughty schoolboys.

Then, one of them suggested to bring in a sniffer dog, which they did. They did not notice Vera filling her hands with pepper as she subsequently walked around the house, dumping pepper onto the floor.

Not long after, the dog began to sneeze and cough. The police thought something was up with the dog and removed him from the house.

The only "evidence" they found was a bottle of clear liquid that they put into the evidence bag, along with two grams of marijuana they had found. The clear liquid was a precursor that

Victor was using to make medical marijuana for his grandmother, who was in Stage 4 of womb cancer. As much as Victor wanted to save his grandmother, the cancer was too far advanced, and the medicine couldn't help her.

Then, with the evidence they collected in a plastic bag, they set up a game of soccer on the driveway using the plastic evidence bag as the soccer ball. After a while they punctured the bottle of precursor, getting everything wet and thereby ruining all of the evidence.

None of them was the sharpest tool in the shed.

Proved when a senior detective told one of them that people tripped when smoking weed. I corrected him that only psychedelics produced that kind of effect on people.

These were drug squad cops who had no idea of what they were talking about.

Then, when I dressed for work, with a senior detective in the room with me as I put my clothes on to make sure I was hiding nothing, I headed out to my car with a junior detective escorting me. Then he took everything out of the boot and left it on the ground for me to put back. I let him know that as he took everything out, it was now his job to put everything back where he found it. He did as he was instructed but somehow lost the lug which held the spare wheel in place, back down into the tyre hole. I instructed him to take the wheel out again, retrieve the lug, put the wheel back, and lock it properly. He did all this without any negative complaints, like a faithful dog.

As I backed down the driveway, I noticed the junior detectives examining the evidence bag they'd destroyed.

I gave them the finger. What a bunch of losers!

We lived in that house for seven years, and when we were first checking out the house, I noticed a strange smell, like that of an old lady wearing too much cologne. When I mentioned the smell to the owner of the house, he quickly changed the subject and began speaking with the estate agent.

I mentioned this to Vera, who'd noticed the smell herself, and she said she'd use some of her "Russian magic" to get rid of the smell and the old lady causing it.

When we moved in, it was one of the first things she did.

90 Taiyul Road was definitely a haunted house and we were to hear many a strange sound at night while in bed. I didn't take much notice of it as I grew up in Mum and Dad's house in Hornsby, which was haunted by an old aboriginal man.

Mum and Dad's house was built on the side of Jack's valley, which in earlier days was a graveyard for indigenous people. When I was really young, I would be disturbed by the sound of someone walking through the house.

On some occasions it would be my Dad as he walked out to the back toilet. Dad would have to cross the lino floor in the sunroom, which gave me the perfect view of anyone walking to the toilet from my bedroom, which had no door on it, just a cutout frame.

But sometimes, it wasn't my Dad, and I'd turn on the light to find that there was no one there at all. When this first happened I checked on Mum and Dad and my sister, all of whom were sound asleep. When I mentioned this to Mum, she said that it was a guardian angel who was checking that I was all right. This immediately relaxed me, and I started to play games with the ghost. I'd wait until I could hear him walking into the sunroom, Lino, then I jumped up and turned on the bedroom light. Sometimes, it was my Dad, but more often than not, there would be no one there. I played this game for years.

But many years later, a friend of Vera's, who was a world-renowned psychic, told me that I had two guardian angels looking after me. I asked if one of the guardian angels was my Mum, and he said it was. Then I asked him if the other guardian angel was my father, and he said no, it was an aboriginal man. This proved to me that my "walking ghost" was my other guardian angel.

One late summer afternoon while living at Taiyul Road, I

was looking for Mork, my cat, as I wanted to feed her dinner. There was nothing under my side of the bed. So I looked under Vera's side of the bed, and there was a tall stack of thin foam sheets, which she had collected from the body board shop at our building in Brookvale. Vera was using the foam sheets for some project she was working on.

While bending over, I inadvertently kicked the foam sheets and the instant that happened, a huge black shadow arose from under my side of the bed, flying up to the height of the ceiling. It saw me, then tipped sideways and flew on an angle out of the room. The thing was easily 7 feet tall, but it didn't scare me. It fascinated me as I'd never seen anything like it before. I had no trouble sleeping on my side of the bed because I scared the shit out of that thing, and I knew it wouldn't be back. I never saw it again while we lived there.

So I researched Shadow ghosts on Google and found that there were three of the things: one black, one white and one gray. I mentioned this to my friend Hamish Sevenoaks, who said he'd seen a gray shadow ghost twice at his studio in Hornsby. When he first saw it, he raced outside to find it and ran into the plumber who was coming to fix a leaking pipe. Apparently, the thing wasn't a black shadow ghost draped in a sheet-like I saw, with no discernible arms, legs or face. What Hamish saw was moving in a strange slow-motion way, and he could see a full human-type body with arms, legs and a face. Later, he saw the same ghost and, once again, had failed to connect with it. This fascinated me as I had no idea that shadow ghosts actually existed.

But I've experienced ghosts, as I've said.

I've heard them and felt them - when the cold dropped in a room when they entered it.

The only ghost I saw was when Christine and I were living at the house on Mona Vale headland, which I was renting from the actor Nick Tate. He was moving to the UK to star in a space-themed series.

Nick was friendly when we went to check out the house - but was completely nude when he answered the door! After the initial shock, later in the interview Nick put a towel around him, and things got back to some kind of normal. We got on quite well and said we'd like to rent the house.

As we were leaving, Nick said, 'Don't worry about Neva.'

Neva was Nick's mother. A well-known musical star who'd died years before.

Okay. Thanks, Nick. Taken on board.

The only time I ever saw Neva was one evening as I was making dinner. I turned and took a step toward the fridge to get something and briefly saw a small woman standing right behind me and glaring at me. It all happened in an instant. But I remember feeling like I'd walked through a mist as I passed through her.

I discovered that Neva never liked me but was fine with Chris and the two kids, Tusyan and Bianca, who were born while living at the house.

Here's another true ghost story. In the early days of my school in 1991, I directed and produced the story of Mary, a friendly ghost who lived at the Alexandra Hotel at Eloura in the Blue Mountains. Malcolm (a former student of mine) and his wife had recently bought the hotel, and he came across a great story for me to produce. It involved Mary, who had been living at the hotel since her murder by her jealous husband in 1888.

Once I heard the story of Mary, I realized it would be a tale well worth making into a short 30-minute film.

Malcolm's wife was using Mary's old room as an ironing room, and every time she left the room to gather more clothes to iron and then returned to the room, a painting on the wall would be on the bed, face down. Whenever she left the room for whatever reason and came back again, the painting was again on the bed. She gave up on the painting and noticed that their dog, a large German shepherd, wouldn't enter the room but would sit at the door and occasionally growl at something in the room. It didn't take her long to figure out who the dog was growling at Mary.

Malcolm did some research on Mary and discovered that she

had been killed by her insanely jealous husband. She had gone to the mountains to recuperate at the Hydro Majestic Spa north of Leura. Her husband caught the train to the mountains and accosted Mary in her hotel room at the Alexandra Hotel. He stuffed her clothes into her bag and tried to remove her from the hotel. A fight between Mary and her husband took place at the top of the stairs in the hotel, and her husband punched her in the face. Mary flew backward down the stairs and broke her neck at the bottom of the stairs. Her husband was arrested, convicted of the murder, and sent to jail.

Working on the script with a student from my school, Cliff, who also played one of the leads in the film "*A Time and a Place*," we came up with the story, which we set in 1988 about a jealous husband and his wife who were staying at the hotel. The story mirrored Mary's fate in 1888, but the twist was that the modern-day husband was found dead at the bottom of the stairs. The same place where Mary died 100 years earlier.

Mary, although harmless, was a bit of a thief. A thing we discovered when my girlfriend Christine, my actor-writer friend Cliff and my production manager Robyn spent a weekend staying at the hotel while

outlining the script. Christine and I slept in Mary's old room, whereas Malcolm informed us if she came to visit, there would be a single knock on the door, and then the temperature in the room nosedived. We were lying in bed, close to sleep, when, sure enough, there was a knock on the door, and the temperature in the room dropped considerably. Christine was poking me in the back, whispering that Mary was in the room. What could I do? *Nothing!* She's a fucking ghost, Chris!

After a while, the temperature in the room rose back to normal. On the same night, while they were asleep, Cliff and Robyn lost the stills camera we were using for location shots. We told Malcolm what had happened, and he set up a search for the camera. It was never found.

So when I arrived at the hotel with the cast and crew a few weeks later, I insisted that the crew and all of our video and audio equipment were based in a new wing of the hotel. A new wing that was built after Mary died. She never ventured into the new wing as it didn't exist when she was here. None of the equipment was stolen, and none of the crew was disturbed by Mary.

A few strange things happened during the recording. The worst of which happened to Andrew, who played the modern-day husband. There was a large bathroom for the use of the crew and cast. On the first day of recording Andrew was shaving and wiping the large mirror to clear it of the steam from the showers when suddenly he saw a woman standing right behind him. She was dressed in 19th-century clothing, and it gave Andrew such a shock that he cut his face with the razor. This mishap added to our recording time as we had to disguise the badly cut cheek so that Andrew looked fine on camera.

The next funny event was all my doing. Cliff was scared of ghosts and it happened during our pre-production weekend at the hotel. Malcolm came up to the room we were working in and said that it was getting pretty cold and we would like a bottle of Baileys to warm us up. Cliff then followed Malcolm downstairs to get the bottle and four glasses. While he was gone, I said to Christine and Robyn that I was going to scare Cliff. I grabbed a white blanket off the bed and hid behind one of the large columns upstairs. When Cliff walked past, I made a ghostly sound and reached out for him. It was like one of the old cartoons when someone saw something scary, and their legs started running down the corridor, but the face was still in the same position, looking at me and screaming until it caught up with the rest of the body. It was absolutely hilarious! But to give Cliff a pat on the back, he didn't drop any of the glasses or the bottle. I've always had this habit of scaring people, and I scared Cliff a beauty!

If you visit the Alexandra hotel in Leura, talk to the bar people, and they will tell you that Mary is still around. One of the young bar attendants I spoke with when in the mountains for the Blue Mountains Music Festival in 2012 remembered me as the maker of the film and said that when she closes the bar at night, she can feel Mary hanging around and even talking to her. Not that Mary ever said anything in return.

So, what are these ghosts?

Are they from somewhere else?

Another dimension?

I've come to believe that they are some sort of *energy*.

I believe that the cities around the world who have been around for more than 400 years and have discovered, that all the old ghosts have disappeared from existence around four centuries after first being sighted.

Easter 2000

Here's another "ghost" story, but in this episode, I scared the crap out of two Jenolan Cave guides who were meant to be scaring the tourists.

During Easter 2000, Vera and I drove up to the Jenolan Caves in Oberon, NSW. The caves are over 340 million years old, the oldest caves in Australia. And the entrance to the Caves is mind-blowing. The caves were first discovered by James Whalan, a pastoralist, but the credit should possibly belong to James McKeown, an ex-convict and possibly an outlaw who was using the valley as a hideout.

Vera and I stayed in a cabin twelve kilometers above the caves. The cabin was very comfortable with heating, a kitchen, and the whole works. Kangaroos were grazing in a large field surrounding the cabins. We spent a lot of time playing with the kangaroos. But as it was starting to get dark, Vera and I returned to the comfort of the cabin. We turned up the heating stove to Thailand-type temperatures and relaxed in our undies. But then Vera had the bright idea of letting in some of the kangaroos. Yeah. *Right.* They would have taken over and we would be sitting outside in our undies! Luckily, I talked her out of that idea.

As I said, I love scaring people, and we undertook a tour of the "haunted" cave. All the other visitors and we were standing around, and the Cave guide said that if we really listened, then we could hear the sounds of some of the ghosts who died in the caves. No one has been recorded as dying in the Jenolan Caves. It was all just a tourist trap. Standing at the back of the visitors, I noticed a long dark tunnel running away into the distance. As I was studying the tunnel a bat flew out of the tunnel straight at my head. I ducked to the right, and the bat flew past me on my left. No one had noticed this, so I took my leave and very carefully walked down the adjoining tunnel to where the noise was coming from. I paused at the entrance to the cave and noticed there were two guides banging saucepan lids together and making ghostly sounds. I jumped out at them and scared the crap out of them. They couldn't believe I'd walked all the way down the dark tunnel just to scare them. One of them offered me a job as a "ghost guide." We had a good laugh.

Women

I've had a few women. Well, not like a porn star's 2,000 plus or something ridiculous. I've made love to around 70 women. I can't remember a lot of their names, but I can picture some of their faces. In 1973, I met Judy Jackson, an American girl. I can't remember how we met, but Judy was a lot of fun. We lived at McMahons Point, across the bay from Luna Park. On some nights, I'd put an album on the turntable, turn off the lights, and Judy and I would sit there looking through the full-length bay windows of our apartment to all the lights and the accompanying yelling and screaming that floated over the bay.

I remember once when Judy and I were driving up the coast and passing the occasional semi-trailer, I suggested to Judy that she should flash one of the truckies. Judy laughingly agreed, and the next truck we overtook, she flashed the driver. He was impressed by Judy's tasty flesh and gave us a long horn blast. We did that every now and then, just for laughs.

Judy and I eventually broke up because she knew I was still in love with Tereza.

Another woman I remember is Sarah Munro. Sarah hailed from Perth, and I met her on the boat when I was deported from South Africa in late 1972. Sarah decided to stay in Sydney for a while at her friend's house, which was located in the inner city. Sarah was a wild child. She loves sex. I mean, so do I, so we got along fine. The friends she was living with were at work all day, so we used the house as a sex pad, and I'd be out of the house before they got home. I was staying with my parents as I'd just returned from overseas.

I remember one-day upstairs in Sarah's bedroom when we were getting into it, and in the back of my mind, I'd registered that the record player downstairs finished one track before the record ended. It was Harry Nilsson's, *Nilsson Schmilsson* album. I knew it well. I had the record. But at the time, I was more concerned with pleasuring Sarah.

When we finally went downstairs later, we found that the thieves had waited until the song ended (one track out from the end) and then stolen the hi-fi system along with some records.

Another time, when Sarah was visiting me at my parents' house, Mum and Dad left the house to buy some shopping. As soon as they left, Sarah was all over me. She wanted to suck my cock, and I was trying to stop her. Mum and Dad would be back soon. I put up quite a fight, but in the end, she got her way – just as my parents drove up! I tried to stop her, and she said: 'I'll bet I can suck you off before they get here.' *Jesus!*

It always took Mum a while to get down the path. She had arthritis but Dad would match her step and guide her down. But now they were almost here! Luckily, Sarah knew what she was doing, and sure enough, she won the bet.

At that stage in my life, I was in love with two women: Alison Price (my first real girlfriend) and Tereza James in South Africa (who I met during my first trip there in 1971.)

Without knowing it, things were about to get *wild*.

Wild Women

When Tereza went back to South Africa in 1977, I eventually became involved with some wild women

and wild times at the house in Narrabeen. These were the late seventies when you only had to look at a woman and show some interest, and you were into bed at the first opportunity. This went on for a while until I met Christine, my second long-term relationship, which eventually provided us with our children, Tusyan, Bianca and Tianjin.

I met Christine and her friend Ren in late December 1977 when the camping ground they were living in behind the house started filling up with holidaymakers. A guy who hung out at the house, Mitchell, said he'd met two girls from Adelaide who were staying at the camping ground with their Alsatian dog, Bo. The girls had to leave Bo alone in the tent when they went to work throughout the week.

Mitchell told them I had a big house. I told Mitchell if their dog Bo, got along well with Buster, they could stay.

The dogs got along just fine. So they moved in.

Along with our jobs and lifestyles, we had some fun times; going to The Lifesaver. Late nights. All that sort of thing.

And then later, when the girls moved up to Noosa Heads in

late 1978, I went up there with Dean (my old house mate at Narrabeen) for a long visit. We all stayed in a house at Noosa Heads.

They were fun times. Good surf. The works.

One time, we went out to a waterfall. It was a perfect day. Jumping into the deep pool below the falls was a buzz.

We went back another time, and we got covered with leaches! It had rained for a few days before we went there that time. Yuk.

Christine and I had some great times, but it felt like a competition sometimes. I was the enemy in some ways because I could never see the light, although I've always respected women and was supportive of their causes and ambitions. So I *could* see the light. I grew up around strong women. My aunties, my female cousins, my Mum and my sister, were a positive education for a young man. So it was strange to be persecuted for all mankind when you had the opposite view.

When Christine and I broke up in December 1994, I went on the rampage again and met some interesting female friends.

One of them (no names here) was very well-off. Worked at a big company. She transferred from the United Kingdom to Australia to help upgrade the Sydney company branch.

I got on well with her, and she wanted to give me a few gifts.

Nothing of any real value. Just a few odds and ends to help me as a film producer on the make: two upmarket shirts and a top-of-the-line Swiss army knife (which I still have today.)

The only problem was that she fell in love with me. I really liked her, but I wasn't in love with her. (I've been in that position before. On the other side, like my friend was now.)

She then went out of her way to change my mind. Eventually, she suggested we go to a swinger's party.

I wasn't sure. I wasn't into hairy Greek guys or older faded-out blondes. I eventually agreed and it was not what I expected. The men were friendly, and their women were sexy. My friend and I had a ball, so to speak. My friend "directed" the process with me and a few of the ladies, and it was very enjoyable indeed. The husbands were encouraging their wives to do this and do that, so I just took their suggestions and went with it.

I went to two swingers parties with my friend, and it was very interesting. My friend paid the admission fee of $100.00 per couple. She was out to impress me. I was nervous when the subject came up, but when we got to the apartment, which was done out well, with a TV showing porno movies, a bar, a spectacular entrance with a big fountain and the people turned out to be nice and friendly; then I finally relaxed a little. And when we got down to it, the actor in me came out.

When we left the last of the two parties we attended, my friend looked at me and said: 'You're in the wrong business. You should have been a porn star!' I laughed as she helped my aching body to the car.

As I said, the actor came out.

Acting

Artists are the progressive free thinkers of the world. Art cannot be bound or shackled by morals, sexism or political correctness. Art is what colors our world. Without it, life would be bland, boring and a gray existence. Artists push the boundaries and expand the context of our lives. If artists were shackled by the conservatives in society, there would be no *Naked Lunch,* no *Fear and Loathing in Las Vegas.* No joy in this bleak world. Only work, work, work, and servitude to the 1% who endeavor to control our thinking and our lives. Artists, by nature, are not greedy people. We don't worship at the altar of the Holy Dollar. For the true artist, it's Art for Art's Sake, and if you can make a living by doing what you love, then you are one of the luckiest people on the planet. If the accumulation of money is the sole purpose of your life, then it is a pretty poor existence. Money is meaningless to a large extent. Money can't buy the truly valuable things in life: health, love, family and friends. You can't take it with you, as they say, and if you spend your entire life grubbing for money, then you will have neglected the real value of life. You do not want to be laying on your death bed wishing you had taken singing, acting or dancing classes, traveling the world, or raising a family that truly loves and supports you. It's *way* too late by then!

Even though I'm not into money and wealth, I'm one of the

richest men of my generation. I have 6 kids and 7 grandkids. We all love and care for each other, and there's nothing better than that. Or richer than that.

When I got back from a trip to America, Canada and Mexico with Christine, I studied as an actor at the New Theater in Newtown. The voice and movement tutor was around 35 to 36 years old. I can't remember her name all these years later, but one of the lessons she taught the class was how to quickly free up your body: 'You stretch as high as you can, then you reach down to touch your toes, moving from 'bone to bone,' then once you've touched your toes, you come back up bone by bone. Then stretch as high as you can.' Do that three times in a row and you're loose as a goose.

The principal teacher at New Theater was Marie Armstrong. Marie was fifty-two years old at the time, with a world of acting and tutoring experience.

When I first joined New Theater, I told Marie that I wasn't interested in acting on stage; I was only interested in the screen. She then let me play down certain roles as if for a camera performance. She said as long as they could hear me and see what I was doing, then it was fine. Most were physically acting anyway. Once, I had to play a seventy-five-year-old man. I was thirty at the time. The old man was sitting with a drink, reminiscing over the tragedy he'd experienced in the Second World War. The class and the tutors were impressed by the performance. Then, I knew I could give the acting a go.

When I graduated in 1981, I spent 8 years working as an actor in film and television programs.

The film and television industry was super busy at the time because of the tax 10BA setup. It meant that if you were cashed up – like a lawyer, medical specialist, business person, whatever – if you invested, say, $100,000, you were secretly hoping that the project wouldn't break even. Then, you can claim the tax benefit of losing your investment, plus an extra tax benefit of 50% on top of that. But hey, as an actor, who cares about the details? It meant a truckload of acting work! I was lucky to graduate then when everything was so busy. It got me a great start.

Working in the industry was challenging. You're always learning something new. I learned a lot about acting and the technical side of acting for the camera. Older people on set also gave me tips.

I acted in a variety of programs, including a couple of big productions.

I got an early start at the Australian Film, Television and Radio School in 1981 when I put my name down on the actors list. Actors were needed to work with emerging directors.

Some of the shoots didn't go as planned. I remember a scene when "my wife and I" were standing outside our "daughter" bedroom, listening to her on the phone.

When they played the rushes back a couple of days later after processing the film (yes, it was a 16mm film), they discovered there was *no* sound recorded. Bummer.

I later saw this mistake again when playing a suspected bad guy on Australia's *Most Wanted* series. I was suspected of stealing a safe and burning down the chemist's shop. But when I asked the policeman, who was on duty with the show, to gain a police perspective. He answered: 'We are not sure if it's an insurance job. He's the last independent chemist in the local suburbs, and he was suffering financially.'

Anyway, we shot the scene between the chemist and me. Then the man playing the chemist had to be at another job. I continued recording with some cutaway shots when I noticed that there were no readouts on the camera sound system mounted on the side of the camera. Instant *panic!*

Then, after considering the problem, the cameraman decided to go to the car park behind the chemist's shop, and I could voice over my lines and he'd do the chemist's lines. So we set up down there, and it was a fiasco. We had black back-sheets over our heads while trying to read our words to the image on a 9-inch monitor. I gave it a good try. But in the end, we couldn't do it.

When the show came on television, my Mum was horrified! She said: 'Everyone will think you're a criminal!'

I said: 'Mum. It's a television series: *Australia's Most Wanted.* I'm an actor. I'm playing a bad guy's role.'

In the end, the series narrator, Brian Marshall, voiced over our section and made it work.

So, not unlike AFTRS, where a trainee director made a mistake, a "professional" production team had stuffed up.

Anyway, I was already established with my acting work at AFTRS since 1981, by working with promising directors and established actors.

I remember one exercise I did. It was with Eva, who was well-established on TV through commercials.

This involved director students showing that they understood how to set up shots and move the camera around. No on-set work. Just the actors acting, and the student directors moving around us showing camera set-ups, angles, close-ups etc., by framing the shots with their hands.

The room was full of film students, actors, tutors and bigwigs at AFTRS. As luck would have it, Eva and I were the first people on the rudimentary set. There was a table, and that was it.

We had to imagine that we were husband and wife and worked up slowly to an argument regarding how to paint the eggs we were decorating.

Up to this point, I was looking for the "space" that Marie Armstrong talked about at New Theater. This is the day I *found* it. I was very nervous about performing in front of all these people. I was an on-camera actor and not used to people looking at me. I slowly began to get into it. The further into it I got, the more it became about just Eva and me. My horizon shrunk. It was like I was going to faint. But at the last minute, the blackness closing in on me stopped. I wasn't even aware of the people in the audience because Eva and I were so involved with the performance. When we finished the scene, I just stood there glaring at her in character. Then I was sure that it was raining. Slowly, I realized that it wasn't raining. It was the people in the room – *clapping!* No one's ever clapped me before. Other than when I was playing Calpernia, Julius Caesar's wife, in a Boy Scouts play. They don't do it on film sets. I was instantly embarrassed. Then Eva took my hand and whispered in my ear: 'Welcome to the *space,* darling.' Then she hugged me, and we were back to our seats.

Then, in 1991, I applied for the Advanced Screen Directors Certificate at AFTRS.

This tough short course was running on the weekends. It was

a new class recently set up - and we were the students to pioneer it. The course was priced at $3,000, but it was only $300 for us as it added additional experience to our directing skills. This was why the course had been set up.

Nine of us were accepted into the course. There were 76 applicants. The course included actor-director Garry McDonald (the disheveled interviewer *Norman Gunston,* who interviewed leading stars in the 7 years the show ran on Channel 7, including interviews with Mick Jagger from the Rolling Stones, Muhammad Ali and Paul McCartney when he was touring with his band, *Wings,* in 1974. Gunston said to Linda McCartney: 'You don't look Japanese' (relating to Yoko Ono.) That brought the house down! Jagger didn't know how to handle Gunston. Is it a joke? Is he serious?

In one recording exercise, I was directing a comedy scene (the scene supplied by Garry.) We were booked into the studio for two hours. We had a short lunch break before we went in, and during that time, Garry and his partner in the scene had everything nailed – the text and the comedic actions. Ready to roll! The amount of lights in the ceiling of Studio 2 was worth hundreds of thousands of dollars. I was using two 800-watt redhead lamps. The massive lighting rig hovers above us, with nothing to do. We were in and out of the studio in record time, just over an hour. The tutor, Di Drew, saw me and asked if I was finished. I said yes. She couldn't believe I'd achieved the results in that time. Di was very skeptical. But when we played back the day's work, my scene worked a treat. Di was impressed by how fast I could work. But I already had 5 years teaching students how to act for the camera. I was used to working quickly and methodically, having fun and getting good results from my students.

I said before that nine of us started the course at AFTRS. One guy - I think he was from Brazil initially - didn't always agree with what Di Drew was saying. But in my mind, he had some really good ideas on how to record a scene. When he didn't turn up one weekend, I wondered what had happened to him. He was an open-minded guy who wasn't afraid to say what he was thinking. I believe he got the boot because of this fact.

Sometimes, the best get left behind.

One time, during a theory session, we had to set up a shot chart – showing camera angles, shot set-ups etc. The class was made up of 8 of us now. There was a woman, and the rest were males.

Half of the class, we'll call them "director-directors" (more interested in camera set-ups than acting) and the other four of us, as "actor-directors," knew how to act and how to find what was needed in the scene. The "actor-directors" could relate to the woman's motivation and brought it to the screen (well, on *paper* in the theory class.) The exercise was done independently.

We were told the story and had to set up a scene with a

woman in the gym at the hospital. She was waiting for her doctor to appear.

The class went into full overdrive with some "director-directors" having as many as 27 camera set-ups for the scene. I felt guilty. I only had 9 set-ups. But what was interesting was that the 4 "actor-directors" had got the emotional content of the scene right. The woman didn't want to see anyone until her doctor arrived and she could go and greet him. We all had the woman shooting at the basket as far from the door as possible. Di went over the results. She observed the actor's position and then the set-ups. She explained that it was for *A Country Practice* and had to be kept simple and effective. As far as setting the scene and having the actor in the right place, the 4 "actor-directors" got it right. We all had the woman standing in the right place for the scene. The 4 "director-directors" failed the exercise. They couldn't understand the woman's motivation. They all had her playing the basket by the door, just killing time and waiting for the doctor. No. She was as far away from the door as possible, hiding out until she saw him.

Di said she had shot that same scene for *A Country Practice* with only two camera-set ups to record the entire scene. Shows the difference between television, and film (where within budget, the director can have all the time they need to get what they want.)

Back in 1986, I realized there were virtually no schools

teaching how to act for the camera. And then I noticed an advert in the Manly Daily paper looking for an acting teacher. The school was situated in Mona Vale, and I lived two suburbs to the north. If I got the job, I'd be ecstatic. So I was interviewed and won the job.

It was called The Mona Vale Film and Television Acting School, owned by a character named Garry Keen.

Once I was up to speed with the business, Garry began to head overseas to Thailand, leaving me to run the studio and an agency with actors like Robert Carlton, Justin Rosniak, and other talented students.

I ran the place professionally, as Garry had instructed me. That meant running a big school along with a talent agency. I did well until Garry got back from Thailand in early 1988 and saw how very few of the students made a big deal of him returning. That's when Garry sacked me.

And then he saw the footage from the short films I made over the Christmas holidays. They looked impressive. Garry fired me before he looked at the footage.

Then, the hide of the man, he rang me at home to ask if I'd like to edit the films. To which I said I wasn't interested, and hung up. I'd already decided to start my own school somewhere around the Dee Why area.

In the end, we found a good place to set up - 173 South Creek Road, Dee Why West. I started the school in mid-July 1988. Around half of Garry's students, when they heard what I was doing, left his school and joined classes at my school, along with the new students I brought into class from newspaper advertisements and an open day at the school.

Some of the top students stayed with Garry, and I'm proud to have taught them to expand their acting skills.

My new school was called The Film and Television Acting Academy. Mum helped me fund the school's set-up costs by mortgaging her house. Mum lent me 10,000 dollars for this purpose. My cynical sister said to Mum: 'He'll never pay the money back!' I told Mum it might take up to two years to pay the loan back, but the school was such a success that I managed to pay back the loan in just nine months. My sister was wrong, as usual.

The school took off well and I let it grow over the first two ten-week terms of classes, assisted by driving a mate's taxi on Friday and Saturday nights. I ceased driving cabs on New Year's Eve 1989 and went into teaching full-time again.

During my time at Garry's school, I'd heard some rumours that Garry was a pedophile, which explained why he kept on visiting Thailand while I was running the business. I didn't put much credence into the rumours until Garry returned in early 1988 with a big scar across the top of his nose. A friend of mine (Malcolm, a former policeman and student at Garry's school) was also in Thailand during Garry's last visit and told me that the wound had come from a young boy's father. Garry had his "date" with the young boy but refused to pay the father. The man attacked Garry with a large piece of wood, causing a wound to his face.

I wasn't sure what to do when I heard that, but luckily, Garry sacked me, and that solved the problem.

Once I learned that Garry was a pedophile, I was determined to start my own school - and this time to do it properly.

Pacific Cabaret

Mum and Dad had quite a bit of community involvement in Hornsby. My Mum did a lot of work for Hornsby Hospital and worked in the canteen at my high school, Asquith Boys High. My Dad was a mover and shaker at Hornsby RSL Club. He was secretary of the RSL for all of the activities the kids were involved with, along with being the Captain of the RSL Air League, teaching kids the beauty of flying and all about airplanes and how they worked.

In the late 1960's, bringing in some extra income for the RSL which was just down the road from the Pacific Cabaret in Ashley Street, Dad set up a regular Saturday night dance at the art deco venue. I was seventeen at the time, and my girlfriend, Alison Price and I wouldn't miss one of Dad's dances. He had some awesome bands lined up, including the La De Dah's Billy Thorpe and the Aztecs. Billy and the band lived locally, and Dad had a good relationship with some of the band members. I'm not a big fan of Thorpie, though; my Dad would have liked to have charged *him* for playing the gig. The only competition was the NSW Police Boys Club, who were holding their dances on the other side of Hornsby, on the new Pacific Highway. Dad had a good rapport with the bands, and as both clubs ran on a Saturday night, Dad always had the pick of who was playing at the Pacific Cabaret, including overseas bands like The La De Dah's, originally from New Zealand.

Something I'll never forget, the keyboardist in The La De Dah's was playing the keyboard with one hand and blowing a sax solo with the other! What a band - and with Kevin Borich on lead guitar, as good as it gets!

The Pacific Cabaret was used for many events over the years of its existence. Built in 1934, it hosted dancing and dancing classes, it was also used as a cinema and, for a little while, as a boxing venue, and eventually into a skating rink in 1975 before closing in 1979.

When entering the Cabaret, you walked past the ticket office and down a long set of red-carpeted stairs to the first landing, where the cafeteria was set up. Directly across from the cafeteria was the band who were playing. You could sit down and have a non-alcoholic drink and see over the heads of the dancers, who were down a short set of stairs to the dance floor below. On the sandstone walls were black cut-outs of palm trees and Hawaiian Hulu dancers. What an exotic and intoxicating setup!

When the Cabaret was demolished in the early 1980s, the new building became a Chinese restaurant.

The classic Art Deco building should have been protected and not been allowed to be sold or demolished. Such a waste of a timeless building.

The Pacific Cabaret

When I was 7 years old, my Mum and Dad took me to the Pacific Cabaret to see the film *The Sea Hawk,* starring Errol Flynn and Olivia DeHaviland. When I left the screening, I wanted to be an actor, just like Errol Flynn. But it wasn't until I returned from touring America in late 1979 that I finally took up the profession by studying to be an actor at the New Theatre.

When I was 10 years old, my older cousins took me to the Hornsby picture show on the old Pacific Highway to see Alfred Hitchcock's film *Psycho.* It scared the hell out of me. I couldn't take a shower with the curtain closed for years after the film, but it made up my mind that I also wanted to be a film director. So I figured that if I started as an actor and learned the craft and the language of the actor, then I would be a far better director by having a good rapport with the people I worked with. And from that young age, that is exactly what I did after four trips to various countries overseas to gain some valuable life experience.

The Bondi Lifesaver

The Bondi Lifesaver was opened on 13 August 1970. Kim Parkes and her husband, John, owned the venue. It was closed due to council interventions on 31 August 1980 - with a huge party at the venue. This was due to complaints from locals about the noise. In 1980 with sound monitor equipment set up every night by the council to monitor sound levels, it was costing the venue anything from $500 to $1000 per night if their decibels were too high - so it simply wasn't viable to continue.

To quote Kim Parkes, one of the owners: 'The Lifesaver was incredibly popular and would hold up to 1500 patrons when we had a big draw card, and on those nights, we could have 25 staff working the bar and two or three bouncers on the door – there was no other venue like it at the time.

I'd give all staff $50 in cash at the end of the night, which was good money for the time, so our staff stayed with us for a long time, which was unheard of in that business.'

The Lifesaver had two massive tanks of tropical fish. The huge tanks were costing $500 a week as each night of the week, a patron would drop some LSD, mandies or speed into the tanks, and the fish would all die!'

When Billy Thorpe first played The Lifesaver, the noise

from the band was so intense that it *also* killed the fish. Well done, Thorpie!

I'd hit the Lifesaver every Thursday and Saturday night, along with occasional Sundays as well. The Lifesaver always had the best bands playing there: Mi-Sex, Ross Wilson's Mondo Rock, X, The Angels, Rose Tattoo, Joe Camilleri and the Falcons, Jimmy and the Boys and AC/DC, for example. Visiting overseas musicians who were touring the country would turn up and join in with the band on stage.

When the place was packed to the max, which it usually was on Thursdays and Saturdays, the sweat from the punters would gather on the ceiling and drip down on us like raindrops. Disgusting, but we handled it.

I remember one night when I was there with surfing buddy Clyde Cameron. I'd had quite a few rums under my belt, but for some reason, I felt completely sober. Then, when something cool was happening on stage, Clyde tapped me on the arm, and I just fell over, taking 7 or 8 people down to the floor with me. They got up and rubbed their filthy hands on my clothing. At least their hands were cleaned on what I was wearing and not on my face or arms.

There was always a cool crowd at the Lifesaver. People who loved their music: I never saw any violence at the venue, but it was reported to have happened, usually through an over-indulgence of alcohol.

Thanks to Sydney's Nanny State, there are very few live music venues happening these days, but Selina's hotel, based at Coogee, is still operating today and drawing a healthy crowd. And so is the Avalon RSL club - which has some great original musical acts playing there every Saturday night.

Back in the 1970s, along with all the good local bands playing locally, there were a lot of overseas bands touring the country as well. In Sydney, the overseas acts were playing at the Hordern Pavillion. I've seen some great bands there, including Lou Reed and John Mayall and the Bluesbreakers. Other bands would play at the Sydney Showgrounds. Bands I saw at the showgrounds were the Rolling Stones and Led Zeppelin, both at the height of their powers in 1972 and 1973.

Along with a mate, Peter Jones, I saw the British band Mungo Jerry playing at the showgrounds in 1970. We were sitting right up the back, well away from the crowd down front, so we could smoke a joint. I was taking a big hit on the joint when, all of a sudden, a hand came down on my shoulder. I looked up, and it was a bloody cop! Then I realized that I knew the man in the police uniform – it was John Hawkins, a printing laborer I knew from my apprenticeship. Hawkins always said he wanted to be a cop, and he'd achieved his dream. When I first noticed his uniform and the panicked look on my face, it tickled him, and he had a good laugh. He sat with us and chatted while we finished smoking the joint.

In the 1990s, I also saw some excellent bands playing at the Hordern Pavillion, including Iggy Pop, and an awesome concert featuring The Dave Grainey Show and the Cruel Sea, with Nick Cave and the Bad Seeds headlining the concert.

The first outdoor rock concert in Australia was the Ourimbah Music Festival on Saturday, 24 to Sunday, 25 January 1970. Many people believe that the first big outdoor concert was the Sunbury Pop Festival in Victoria. But that was on Australia Day in 1972, and Ourimbah was the first big outdoor rock concert held in Australia, inspired no less by the success of the Woodstock festival in 1969. Ourimbah had a great lineup of performers, including Max Merritt and the Meteors, Billy Thorpe and the Aztecs, Tamam Shud, Jeff St John, Tully, Wendy Saddington, Doug Parkinson, the Nutwood Rug Band and the Chain.

When we drove into the festival, Ian Kreger (Goliath) and I were in Peter Jones' (the Wog) beige 1967 Holden panel van. Our surfboards were out of sight in the back of the panel van, and the parking attendants thought we were roadies bringing in stage equipment, and they just kept waving us forward - all the way to the back of the stage! Perfect. We parked right there at the rear of the stage with access to the car whenever we needed it - without the long walk out to where all the other cars were parked.

On our first evening at the festival, I had a white blanket in the car and decided to get it. It was getting cold. When I returned to my spot at the front of the stage, a woman approached me and asked could share my blanket. Not a problem. We ended up back in the car. But there was something slightly wrong with her. Up until then, I'd only had three years of sexual experience and didn't know what the problem was.

It was Gonorrhea. I discovered that a few days later while at work in the printing factory at North Rocks. I was standing in the men's toilets with a group of printers and laborers watching. I squeezed my dick, and out came some yellow gunk, sort of like cumming, but it was yellow fluid!

They all screamed – *OUT LOUD!* 'Oh my God, he's got the Jack!'

Yes. Well... Seven injections of antibiotics, and I was fine again - after a needle a day for 7 days running! *Ouch!*

And with my friends, Wog and Goliath, hanging at the lower window of the hospital seeing everything that was going on, only added to the madness. Yeah. Been there. Done that.

I also had the crabs, too, once from wearing a pair of friends' jeans when he had the crabs to get crabs from a girl. That was it for my sexual STDs. It wasn't hard-core syphilis. You didn't hear of anyone dying from syphilis back then. These were more light-weight STDs, like gonorrhea or crabs. Not a bad record. Especially for those times.

Music was always there to help you through life. It meant everything in those days. On the radio, Bands playing concerts; on my turntable, or my friends' turntables. Music played at airports in Europe - I remember hearing some tracks from the album *Tapestry* by Carole King in late 1971 in Europe somewhere.

And when Paso (an Aussie friend I met in Durban) and I were in Portugal, there was all the latest music playing through loud speakers on the beach.

Perfect.

Music has played a huge part in my life, and without music, the world would be a drab and boring place.

Teaching

Acting isn't an easy craft to learn, but it's not rocket science. I've learned so many things over the years as an acting teacher and have worked with some fabulous students, some of whom have become life-long friends.

I was never a teacher/director who was pedantic. I'm always willing to listen to what students have to say about a scene or how it should be recorded, no matter how old they are.

Acting is all about developing your essential life skills - confidence, self-esteem, and collaboration.

I've trained some actors who've won major awards, along with some who've acted in or produced winning festival films, including the Short Black Film Festival, Tropfest, and SF3.

In 1996, I decided to close the school for a little while so I could rename it the Screen Actors Workshop and rejig the curriculum. I never liked the word *Academy,* and I believed the new name reflected the school's aims much better.

My school's been through three recessions and the GFC over the past thirty-six years, and we're still going, so we've done something right.

The Screen Actors Workshop has won two Outstanding Educational Service Awards, along with being a finalist in the Australian Small Business Champion Awards.

As I've mentioned, I trained as an actor at New Theatre and then spent eight years performing in a variety of film and television productions before going behind the scenes and studying at The Australian Film, Television and Radio School.

Some of my film industry credits include directing the Swearing-in Ceremony of Police Commissioner Peter Ryan for the NSW Film Archives, corporate videos for clients as diverse as MYOB and the Queensland Department of Primary Industries, numerous music clips, around 60 short films, and the documentary films *Funnel Webs* (7 Network, Beyond Distribution) and *Boomers and Slackers* (GDTV South Africa.)

I've been involved with the SmartFoneFlickfest International Film Festival since its inception 10 years ago. My school is a sponsor, and I'm one of the judges. The two women running the festival, Angela and Alison, certainly know what they're doing. From its early start, the festival has become the leading SF3 festival in the world. And it's all thanks to their dedication and their love of film.

Presenting the Best Actor Award

Alan Nurthen

Funnel Webs Documentary

Funnel Webs was a hit documentary and sold to over 40 countries and territories. It cost me 4 years of my life to make the film; constantly running out of money and chasing investments took a lot of time and energy. But at the end of the day, once the program was aired on Network 7, I sold the film to The Australian Museum Shops nationwide and to two-thirds of the nation's high schools. The documentary potentially saved a lot of lives and was well worth the effort.

Whenever a funnel web spider was sent to The Australian Reptile Park near Gosford for antivenom milking, a friend who was head of the department would ring me and arrange for me to pick up the specimen. I discovered that a male funnel web spider would only last a month or so in captivity, but the female could live for 20 years.

I saw a lot of strange spiders - a bright red funnel web and an albino funnel web.

I ran into a guy one time when I was collecting food for the spiders, and when I told him what I was doing, he tied up his dog and ended up catching more cockroaches than I did! As I mentioned, all the work I put into the documentary was well worth the effort as it demystified the dreaded spider and gave people hope that they would live if they were bitten by a male funnel web spider. All thanks to the antivenom produced by scientist Struan Sutherland at

84

the Commonwealth Serum Laboratories in Victoria. Struan is an Australian hero as no one has died from a funnel web spider bite since the antivenom was released, and Struan was always there to help doctors twenty-four-seven cope with funnel-web spider bites.

On the first application of antivenom to a patient, Struan was on the phone with the doctor who was administering it to the bite victim. When the doctor told Struan he had already given the victim three shots of antivenom, Struan said: 'Well, he's going to die anyway, so just keep shooting him up with the stuff.' On the sixth injection, the man recovered completely. The antivenom was also used on a nine-month-old baby, who recovered in less than 24 hours. The baby mentioned was Julia Burnside, who I had interviewed along with her mother, Wendy, for the documentary. Many years later, Wendy and her 15-year-old daughter Julia turned up at the acting studio, and Wendy booked Julia into a teen class. There was something familiar about them. Then I recognized both Julia and Wendy and told them that I'd interviewed them for the film I made. They were shocked and said that, yes, they remembered the interview. Wendy said that Julia was close to death, but thanks to the antivenom, she fully recovered in just one day and was released from emergency care the following day. Needless to say, Struan was her hero because, without the antivenom, Julia would have died.

The DVD slick for Funnel Webs

The first time I saw a funnel web was when I was around 7 years old. I had a tummy ache and woke up in the middle of the night and turned on my bedroom light. I saw a female funnel web coming from somewhere in the sunroom and heading for my bed. As it passed under the bed, I leaned over and noticed a hole in the wall, which the spider had disappeared into. The spider had obviously come up from Dad's workshop under the house.

The spider fascinated me. And it was not until many years later that I made my documentary on the funnel web spider.

When I went to attract a pre-sale for the documentary, I had a 10-minute short to promote the pre-sale along with a script. I assumed it would take ages for the networks to get back to me and was surprised when four of the big five television stations, 7, 9, 10, and SBS, approached me the next day by fax – all of whom wanted the program! I had the right program at the right time. Unbelievable!

The 7 networks offered me the best deal, $40,000, for the right to screen the program twice. When I let 7 know that the 9 network was committed to buying the program, they upped the pre-sale price to $45,000. I then quickly faxed them that they had a deal.

It wasn't until months later that the ABC got back to me and instructed that a 30-minute program would suit them fine. Way too late, ABC! The deal was signed, and the program was well underway at that time.

Burning of the Bush

Before I got into the Funnel Webs documentary, I had an incident with spiders in late 1982. The house we lived in behind Newport was surrounded by scrub and bush. I saw a huge female funnel-web spider when mowing the back lawn. I panicked. Chris and I had two young children to raise.

It's not a good look with funnel webs around.

So I bought some petrol and started to pour petrol down each of the holes I could find in the front garden. I didn't realize that these were good spiders - trapdoors, who have nests in broad daylight when funnel webs go for much darker places to nest. I didn't know that trapdoors have exit holes built into their nests. The next thing I knew, there was a rushing sound, and I looked down to see a flame exiting from the exit hole in a nest - right next to the petrol can! I just managed to drop the can and jump aside when the whole front yard caught fire. It made a massive *BOOM!* I rushed for the hose to put it out. The woman neighbor over the road watering her front lawn couldn't believe it when the hedge caught fire.

Later the next day, at Newport to pick up the Sunday papers, a few people asked me if I'd heard the loud *BANG* ... I said yes. But didn't know what it was about.

I had a good laugh with friends and family after that little episode.

Luckily, it was summer, and the hedge grew back quickly.

The Industry

During my teaching career, I have trained numerous Gold and Silver Logie winners, a BAFTA winner, a nominee for a Broadway-World Best Actress in a Touring Musical, and two Best Supporting Actor Academy award nominees. My teaching career dates from 1986, and I'm proud of the effective and useful life skills I've passed on to my students over the years. When studying for acting and then thrust into the industry, and having two kids already, I was driving taxis on Friday and Saturday nights, along with any acting jobs I could get and writing for the international surfing/travel magazine every month with the legendary Nick Carroll as editor of the Tracks department. I was one of the action-adventure writers at Tracks from 1983 to 1987. I was writing 2000 words for each occasional story that was printed. Then I came up with a 12-part story, "Tales of the Owl," which was a big hit with the readers. Nick's wife, Wendy, was the artist at the magazine, and she created a very effective logo for each of the twelve issues the story ran in.

The artwork for Tales of the Owl

Tracks proved that I could deliver work under a deadline. Tracks ran 2000 words per issue, 24000 for the twelve issues of "Tales of the Owl." Once published in Tracks over the next year, I expanded the story to 28,000 words and sold the story to Newsprint Novels in Victoria.

Driving cabs taught me heaps. I saw everything. I experienced almost everything. The passengers treated you like a doctor. In other words, you wouldn't tell anyone what they said or did. 'He's a cab driver. He's cool.'

After following my instincts/intuition when driving cabs, including two that could have turned the worst. Well, three, actually.

Once, I picked up a drunk at the Avalon taxi rank. I had "Not for Hire" on the roof sign, but this guy just wanted to get home. I was looking up the location in the street directory when he jumped in and told me where he lived. I told him I wasn't for hire, and he just kept going on about me taking him home. I finally gave up and drove the short trip to his home. Then, along the way, he started abusing me. Calling me a poofter, trying to stir me up. Along the way, he threw down the two-dollar fare, and I brushed it off the seat. Told him I didn't want his money. Then he left the money there and got out of the cab when we stopped. Then he hauled off and gave the passenger door a good kick.

All I could think of was Greg Short, my mate who owned the taxi. I wasn't happy explaining how it happened. I bent down with my torch to examine the door (it was a long dark street at the back of Avalon), and as I stood up, he threw a roundhouse punch at me. I ducked back, and he followed the swing all the way through and plunged down the steep embankment. It was hilarious! I couldn't see anything due to the darkness and all the scrub covering the steep drop.

I laughed and yelled out: 'Are you okay?' Then, slowly, I could hear he was still alive as he stumbled around in the scrub at the bottom of the drop. 'You, stupid poofter!' he called out in his drunken voice.

The other two incidents involved a gun being pointed at me and a mob of guys running toward me in a dead-end alley in the city.

The gun could have been a joke. I wasn't sure at the time. It happened at Neutral Bay. I was stopped at a set of lights, and I looked over at the car stopped next to me in the other lane. The passenger lifted a gun and pointed it at me. I thought it was a joke, and I burst out laughing. The guy with the gun then lowered it and grinned back. Then the lights turned green, and we were off. What the man with the gun did later that day was up for grabs. Maybe the gun was for a bank hold-up? Who knows? They took off at the green light, so I didn't have time to question him or to get the registration of the car they were in.

The alley scene was when I stopped at somewhere quiet in the city to take a piss. I was just finishing when I noticed a mob of people at the entrance to the alleyway. They were muttering among themselves, and then when they saw I'd seen them, they charged me. I jumped into the cab and gunned it backward out of the alley. These guys meant harm, robbing me at the least. I wasn't concerned about them, only me. I didn't care who got in the way of my backward retreat. Luckily, no one did. Although in my rush out of there, those in the way quickly flattened themselves against the alley wall.

Alan Nurthen

Trust Your Instincts

Speaking as an experienced actor, I'd say trust your instincts. Your instincts shouldn't let you down. I've gone with a feeling I had when the camera was rolling, and my instincts and intuition never let me down. I'd get an idea and add it to the performance, and it usually worked.

I'll tell you another story, a very creepy story about how I learned to trust my instincts and intuition. My gut reaction, if you like. It was July 1979, and my girlfriend Christine and I were six weeks into our travels around America, living out of a van we bought in San Francisco. We were in Port Arena in far northern California, and we woke one morning to a beautiful blue sky after days of foggy conditions. We asked the lovely old lady we'd been staying with for a couple of days if she could point us in the direction of the nearest beach.

We followed her directions to a small car park beside large sand dunes, whereupon we gathered our gear and started up the nearest dune. We walked over a few sand dunes and noticed that the ocean didn't appear to be getting any closer, so we pushed on for another twenty minutes, and still, the sea was far off in the distance. It was like an optical illusion. From our vantage point on top of a dune, I noticed that it appeared very windy on the still faraway beach as the ocean was full of white caps. So, we decided to lay out our beach towels at the base of a dune. We'd been there for around an hour or so when wispy streaks of fog began to roll in, and my girlfriend decided to head back to the van. I told her I was going to stay a while longer and that I'd meet her back there. Fifteen minutes after she left, I heard this sound way off in the distance, and whatever it was, it was getting closer and closer! Whatever it was, it sounded like it was heading straight for me.

You know that sound the Grim Reaper's scythe makes in those old AIDS television ads? That swoosh swoosh swoosh sound? Well, that's exactly what it sounded like, and it was getting closer and closer and louder and louder. When it was right on top of me, I sat bolt upright just as a huge Jack rabbit flew over the top of the sandhill beside me, smacked down next to me, and leaped clear over the top of the next sand hill.

My first thought was of my girlfriend and that she was in grave danger. I immediately gathered up my belongings and hightailed it out of there as fast as I could. I finally made it to the top of the last dune, completely drained. The side door on the van was open ... and there she was, sitting there making sandwiches.

I started rattling on about the Jackrabbit and continued to do so for months as we traveled across America. There was something surreal about the whole event that just wouldn't let go of me.

Five months later, with Christine threatening violence if I

ever mentioned the bloody rabbit again, we were sunbathing on Coco Beach in Florida when I came across an article on page 9 of the local paper.

I was stunned when I read it and quickly passed the paper to my better half. All I said was, 'Remember the Jackrabbit?' I watched her as she read the article, and although we were heavily tanned, I saw her literally turn white in front of my eyes. Her hands were shaking when she lowered the newspaper, and she said in a shaky voice that she'd never doubt me again.

The article stated that the local police had discovered nine bodies stuffed into the sand hills at Point Arena, all of whom were murdered between May and August 1979. We were there in July.

As far as I was concerned, the Jackrabbit was warning me away because the killer or killers were either in there doing their foul deeds, or we were lying right next to some poor departed soul.

As I mentioned, as an actor, good instincts are vital. After all, you can quickly spot talent through the choices and decisions the actor makes. And those choices have a lot to do with solid research and good old gut instinct.

America

America, like any country, has some outstanding people and the usual dregs. The biggest drag on America is the National Rifle League (NRL.) Thanks to the Constitution all Americans can arm themselves, and this leads to a lot of problems. The NRL basically runs the government and can dictate their wishes to those in power. No wonder there is a constant repetition of shootings in schools and other public places. And what does the NRL do about it? Absolutely nothing! It's all about greed and the profits they are making from arms sales to the paranoid and fearful Americans.

Drive through any small town in the USA, and you'll see large advertising signs outside of gun shops. "Protect your family. Buy a gun."

Only the NRL can construct a pink AK47 and pitch it to young girls. They'll sell a gun to anyone. No wonder the country is so unsafe!

During our trip around America, we ended up in Virginia on the East Coast. We were parked in the car park of a 7-Eleven just enjoying ourselves. Christine and I were playing a game of backgammon. The 7-Eleven was out in the sticks. The ocean was hidden behind the scrub surrounding a creek, and the only noise was the croaking of frogs. We were sitting on a brick fence that allowed us to have one foot touching the ground near where the van was parked and a 10-foot drop on the other side of the wall. On the ground at the bottom of the 10-foot drop, you could see there used to be an old building there sometime in the distant past, as there were patches of broken-up concrete still littering the ground.

While we were playing backgammon, two guys arrived on black Harley Davidson motorbikes. They started a conversation with us and were stoked when they heard we came from Australia. They were navy guys stationed at a big base in Virginia. The navy guys went into the 7-Eleven and bought a bottle of strawberry wine, which they shared with us. We hit it off and were having a great time. It was a quiet location and when a car happened to pass by, which was rare, you'd automatically look up at the road.

After a while, we heard a car approaching, and this time, the car stopped in the middle of the road. There appeared to be only the driver in the brightly colored orange van, and he yelled out what sounded like: 'Would you like to buy some speed?'. I shook my head and waved him off.

The road must have had a looping road connected to it as 15 minutes later, the van came back heading in the same direction, but this time it pulled into the vacant lot beneath us. The driver jumped out of the car and started pointing his finger at us and screaming obscenities. I noticed that Christine was standing right beside one of the navy guys, and I could see him whispering to her. The other navy guy sitting opposite me on the wall whispered: 'Don't say anything. Don't move.' After running out of obscenities, the driver of the van turned around and punched the hood of the van so hard that I was sure he'd broken his hand. Then, taking no notice of the damage he'd caused to his hand, he went to the driver's side of the van, and I saw someone in the back of the van part the curtains and pass him a shotgun. He then pointed the gun at us and continued raving obscenities at us. I was convinced this was my last moment on earth, but luckily, after a few minutes, he threw the gun into the van and drove off.

We were incredibly shaken up by the ordeal, and the two navy men couldn't apologise enough for what had happened to us. They couldn't believe we'd traveled all the way to America and had a run-in with a crazy gun-toting lunatic.

Then, to top it all off, a few minutes later, a fat donut-addicted cop turned up, went into the 7-Eleven, and then returned to advise us that the person working at the 7-Eleven was afraid we were going to rob him! I then explained to the cop what had just happened to us, and he wasn't at all concerned about the incident. He was only concerned about the man working in the 7-Eleven.

Hey, blockhead, don't worry about a deranged man with a shotgun harassing people. The cop didn't even ask for a description of the van or the driver. Unbelievable!

Welcome to America - "Home of the brave, land of the free." Yeah. *Right.*

While we were on the East Coast of America, looking for waves, we stumbled into the competition for the East Coast American Surfing Championships. It was at Cape Hatteras, one of the islands off the coast of North Carolina.

I couldn't go surfing where they were holding the contest, so I went down the beach a bit and did some free surfing with some American guys. When we got to talking between waves, and they discovered I was an Australian and came from North Narrabeen Beach in Sydney (renowned as one of the world's best sand bank breaks), I was the international toast of the day.

Later, some of the guys invited Christine and me to a party they were having at a swank beach house. When we left the beach later in the day, Christine developed a really painful ear infection. Her face started turning a greenish colour. I drove her to the local hospital and waited until they'd sorted her out.

By the time she was released, it was two in the morning. So we both missed an awesome party. Luckily

Christine was getting much better over the next couple of days, so we laughed at missing the party by then.

The West Coast of California in 1979 was a different story

when surfing. It still is today. Unlike the clean East Coast, there were oil rigs off the coast in California. The globs of oil floating in the water would turn the wax on your surfboard black from lying on the board and paddling. There were feet scrapers set up on the beaches so you could scrape the oil off the bottom of your feet.

And the greedy heads in Australia want to set up oil drilling rigs between Woolongong and Newcastle! They should be sent to California to see the result! Disgusting. Nothing but "make the money now and fuck the future." Unfortunately, we have to share the planet with people like these.

When we arrived in San Francisco and settled in, we bought an old Chevy van from a band's roadie. He had a baby on the way and didn't need the van anymore. We called the van "Bertha" and travelled 17,000 miles (27,358 kilometers) in her. Before we left to go home, I sold the van to a guy in San Francisco for the same price I paid for it. The van only caused trouble once, and it happened while we were still on the west coast. It turned out that the carburetor was loose, and while we were stranded by the side of the road, a young man driving a black Porsche 911 pulled over and asked what was wrong. As it happened, he was a motor mechanic. He grabbed a screwdriver, tightened the carburetor, and then invited us back to his house for dinner and a sleepover. A lovely man, and his house was absolutely awesome. Like a lot of houses, it was made from wood, and when we went up a ladder to the top bedroom, we discovered that the tilted ceiling was made from glass. We could lay in bed and just stare at the stars above us.

Months later, while we were in the Deep South, I got talking to a tall black man while we filled our cars at a service station. He noticed the California plates on the van. He started a conversation and learned that we were from Australia. He was driving a big modern car, and when I told him we were driving around the United States, he said that he wouldn't drive to the next state as he was afraid his car would play up. He couldn't believe how far we'd come in our old van.

At another service station in the deep south, I was filling the van when a bunch of hillbillies pulled in next to me. They were driving a flatbed truck similar to the one the *Beverley Hillbillies* drove in the TV show. The man filling the old truck seemed to be around my age, 30 years or so, but it was hard to guess his age as hillbillies aged quickly due to the harsh lives they led. At the back of the truck, sitting on all of their personal belongings - as they were obviously moving from one shack to another shack - was a huge German shepherd dog. In the truck cabin, there was a young boy sitting by the window with an old granny next to him. When the boy spotted me, he said: 'Hey, mister? Mister? Pat ma dog. Pat ma dog.' Yeah, right. If I want to lose my hand! While the boy was speaking to me, the granny was shaking her head in a 'no, don't do it' way, and when the kid turned around to see her, she just sat there and stopped shaking her head. The boy turned to face me again and continued his spiel: 'Pat ma dog. Pat ma dog.' The granny shook her head again, and the kid turned to scope her. She immediately ceased shaking her head. This went on until the driver of the car returned from paying for the fuel, and they took off.

It wasn't the first time I'd seen Hillbillies, and they seemed polite enough. It was the rednecks that could be a problem, and I'd seen plenty of them in the deep south. While we were in Florida, we met a guy named Chuck. Christine could see right away that Chuck was on the way down. He was friendly enough, but there was this deep undercurrent of loss in his life, and it wouldn't be too long before he cracked, picked up an automatic weapon, and went berserk in a supermarket complex. Chuck had lost a lot in his life so far. He was around my age at the time, 30 years old or so. His girlfriend left him for another man, he'd lost his job, and his parents were recently killed in a car crash. I felt he was fairly safe when we met him and had no problem living at his house for a week or so. All Chris wanted to do was get out of there as quickly as possible. As an aspiring actor-writer, Chuck was a good study, though, so I was happy to stay for a while.

The way we met Chuck was interesting, as I'm sure he thought that I was psychic after what happened. We were driving along some darkened road in Florida somewhere when I noticed him hitching. Chris and I were going out to dinner, and when I pulled the van over, Chris climbed into the back to get changed. When Chuck got into the van, he inadvertently kicked one of Chris's shoes out of the passenger door. It wasn't until Chris climbed back in front and sat on the engine cover to search for her shoe that we realised that Chuck must have kicked the shoe out the door when he got in. I had a pretty good idea of where I picked Chuck up, so I did a U-turn and went looking for the shoe. When I got to the place where I thought I'd picked him up, I pulled over and did a quick search. Within a minute, I was back in the car with the missing shoe in my hand. This little exercise blew Chuck's mind! He couldn't believe that I'd found the shoe so quickly and easily. From then on, I was in Chuck's good book and he couldn't do enough to help us out.

While staying at Chuck's, he invited us to come with him to the Florida swamp to meet some of his friends. The men he knew lived in a small shack deep into the swamp, and they seemed okay. But one of them, a gnarly little guy, just looked at me the whole time we were there. Not saying anything. Just staring at me. When we left, I made it to the bottom of the small set of stairs outside the cabin when he approached me. He was quite aggressive and asked me why I spoke so funny. I turned and faced him and said the reason I spoke so funny was that I was an Australian, and we all had that accent. Before he could have a go, I gave him a push, and he fell backward onto the stairs. I turned and walked casually back to Chuck's car. The redneck got up, gave me a dirty look, and went back inside the cabin.

In the deep Southern states of America, Chris and I met a young African-American friend. We hung out for a couple of days, and he showed us around his town as best he could. Then Chris and I moved on and hit the road again. But the looks we got from the local people were frightening. They couldn't understand why we were with this black man.

I'm not saying that everyone who lives down there is racist. They're not. But the racism there can definitely make you angry at the narrow-mindedness of it all. This is where the Klu Klux Clan was started, to say the least.

Early in our trip, while still on the West Coast of America, I was in a supermarket when this large woman reached up to get something on a higher shelf. Then she fainted, collapsed on top of me, and pinned me to the floor. Then she *pissed* on me! Luckily, the guy at the checkout was a medical student and knew exactly what to do. He got her air tanks from her car, and while he was setting her up, I went to the toilet to clean myself up as best I could.

America? What can you say? Every day feels like a week, and every week feels like a month. There's just so much going on over there.

Middle America is highly religious and super conservative, but in other states, many have this attitude that they could sell anyone anything. They even believe they could sell us the Harbour Bridge!

The opposite is true. In many ways, Chris and I scammed our way around America using our skills and life experiences to do the most outrageous things.

One day, when we were in New York, we decided to hit the beach and swim. The beach was incredibly crowded with pale-skinned New Yorkers who had no understanding of the ocean. Except in one small part of the beach, the ocean was as flat as a tack. But down the beach, there was a perfect wedge set-up where 6 to 8-foot waves were breaking in deep water just a few meters from the sand. What luck! I ran down the beach and jumped into the waves. As soon as I jumped in, the next wave picked me up; I spun around and went over the falls into deep water. As I surfaced, the next wave picked me up again, and I was doing the washing machine thing. Up the face of the wave, spin around and down with the crashing wave into the deep trench. Over and over again. After a while, I could hear a whistle blowing and saw a lifeguard on the beach desperately waving me in. When I walked up the beach, he had a go at me for surfing away from the flags. Then he realised that I wasn't some crazy local but an Aussie who could actually body surf. He told me that even though the water was so shallow, except at the wedge, you'd have to walk out for a while before the waves even touched your knees. But the problem was the locals had absolutely no understanding of the ocean, and he was also looking after the beach by himself. He said these people would drown in a bathtub if left on their own. I volunteered to help, and we went back to the lifeguard station, where he gave me a lifeguard cap, a lifeguard vest, and a whistle. I had a ball, whistling and moving my hand in the direction I wanted the crowd to move in the water. The sole lifeguard said that if I got too hot and wanted a swim, then I should head down to the wedge and cool off in the powerful waves for a while.

Chris and I spent the entire day helping the lifeguard and knocked him off when he did at the end of the day.

Sure, I've made a few rescues on my surfboard back home, but when I told the lifeguard that I was a lifeguard from Narrabeen, NSW, he didn't question it and was only too happy to have the help of someone who knew the ocean. That was just one of the scams we pulled off - and we would do it whenever the opportunity arose.

Many hitch hikers on the roads we travelled driving around the USA would have a "catch theme" to help you out if you picked them up. You'd see people with a boom box, pointing to it: 'Pick me up, and you'll have music to drive to!' Or they'd be making out to smoke a joint in the hope of being picked up. We never picked up any of them, but we did pick up hitchhikers who looked friendly and cool.

When I was around 9 or 10 years old, I loved checking out

the empty houses and businesses that were closed due to the construction of The Westfield Plaza in Hornsby. I was always fascinated by empty houses. I'd walk through the houses and try to imagine who lived in them and their respective lifestyles.

Since then, I've had a mission of entering empty houses and checking them out. No one would ever know I'd been in there as I never left a mess, and you couldn't see that someone had broken in. I'd find an unlocked window, or the front door wouldn't be locked, and I'd be in there checking the place out.

In the deep south of America, we stopped by the side of the road in Mississippi next to a large cotton field. We got out of the van and started picking a small amount of cotton. At the far end of the cotton field, there was a really frightening-looking old house. It had turrets on the roof, and the house was boarded up with thick wooden planks. The planks were nailed into place to keep something *inside* the house, not to stop people from entering. When Chris saw the house, she shuddered and said: 'I bet you won't go exploring in that place!' She was dead right about that!

Childhood Mishaps

I was always a bit of a wild child. Kids can be vicious. And we could be vicious toward the only member of our Silvia street gang who didn't really fit in with the rest of us: poor old Helmet Moldners. Being the lead shit-stirrer of the group, I was always coming up with plans to humiliate Helmet.

One of our favourite hangouts was the bridge and the creek and the steep dirt road that ran down toward the bridge, the lower property of the Watson's, the neighbours who lived behind our house at the far north end of the valley. One day, when we were riding a tricycle down the steep road and over the bridge, causing the wooden planks on the bridge to vibrate as we rode over them, I talked Helmet into having a go on the little bicycle. He was hesitant at first, but I kept at it, and eventually, reluctantly, he sat on the bike. Once he was on, I gave him a big push, and he hurtled down the road toward the bridge. He couldn't control the bike, missed the bridge, and ploughed into the bamboo on the left side of the bridge. He ended up in the creek, which wasn't that deep, and crawled out, dragging the bike behind him. We all thought it was hilarious. Not so much Helmet, who was still shaken by the fast ride down the hill. Less than a week later, when a small group of us were back at the bridge again with the tricycle in tow, we noticed a red-bellied black snake emerge from the bamboo and slither under the bridge.

Luckily, the Helmet wasn't with us. He'd have a heart attack if he saw the snake!

Another time, at the lower end of Silvia Street, where Helmet and his mum and dad lived, there was a giant oak tree. We hassled Helmet to climb up the tree in search of cicadas, and each time he stopped and looked down, we'd encourage him to go higher. He got so high up in the tree that eventually, a branch he was standing on collapsed, and he fell all the way to the ground – luckily, hitting a few branches on the way down, breaking his fall. The accident broke his pelvis, and Helmet spent a lot of time in hospital recovering.

It wasn't the only bone broken at that end of the street. Silvia Street was flat in front of my house, but when you walked to the corner of Sylvia Street and Watson's Avenue, only two houses south, the road dipped down nicely and made the perfect "wave" to ride on a skateboard – something I did every day after school and on weekends when I was 13 to 17 years old, on my Midget Farrelly skateboard and "surfed" all the way to the end of the street near Helmet's house. Then, to the left, at the dead end of Silvia Street, was Roper Avenue, which ran up a steep hill. It was on this hill that we rode our billy carts, and one day, my cousin Ronny had an accident and broke his leg. We always had a lot of respect for Roper Avenue Hill. It could be deadly.

At the top of the hill stood an old house occupied by the

grandmother of a friend of mine who lived at the end of Roper Avenue. When we got a little older, we loved playing on the grounds of the house. There was an old barn surrounded by scrub, and the property was huge. It was built during the Boer War in South Africa, and the locals were fearful that the Boers would attack Australia. As if! The Boers didn't even have a navy, let alone any ships! The grandmother had requested hidden escape tunnels to be installed in the house because of the paranoia over an invasion by the Boers. There was one tunnel upstairs in the lounge room, which led downstairs into the kitchen and was disguised by a crockery cupboard. Like I said, the old house was the perfect hangout, and we'd play there whenever we felt like it. The grandmother encouraged us to play outside because her grandson, being our age, always played with us.

Probably the nastiest thing I ever did to Helmet occurred in the lead-up to Christmas when we were both about 8 years of age. I had a red phone, which my sister had given me for her birthday, and I pretended it was plugged straight into Santa Claus's phone. When all of the gang were lined up waiting to hear what Santa Claus said regarding their presents, via me on the red phone, when it came to Helmet, I paused for a little while and then told Helmet that Santa Claus said he'd been a bad boy and wouldn't be getting any presents that Christmas. Helmet lost it and started crying and ran home. We all thought it was hilarious until Helmet turned up at my place with his mum and dad. They were furious, and it took my parents a while to calm them down. Once again, I was in the shit and was banned from Watson's house, along with playing in the street with the other kids for two weeks.

Helmet, at the age of 13, became a bit of a local hero. On Sunday, 6th May 1962, 12-year-old Johnny Myers of Innes Avenue, Hornsby, drowned at The Fishponds. When walking in single file around the edges of The Fishponds with Johnny, a kid from my class at school, Johnny fell and landed on a ledge six feet down. Johnny tried to cling to the ledge but fell another 4 feet into the water. Helmet knew his friend could not swim, so he dived, fully clothed, into the water and tried to drag the struggling Myers to the bank. Helmet told the police Myers had slipped from his grip and disappeared under the surface. Myers was a well-liked boy and a talented cricketer with the Thornleigh Cricket Club. Later that year, the Hornsby Ku-ring-gai Cricket Association named the award for the Junior Club Champion, the Jonathan Myers Memorial Trophy, which is still awarded to this day.

A big search was launched looking for Myers body, and it was three days later that he was found floating in The Fishponds.

The funeral for Johnny Myers was heartbreaking. I sat there watching his parents and tried to imagine what they were going through. Johnny was only 12 years old, and they'd lost their only son. I was deeply saddened by the whole affair. A terrible accident had robbed me of a great friend. Johnny was just starting his life at the age of 12 - and now he was gone forever.

Hornsby Scouts

I learned a lot about surviving in the bush when I was a member of the Scouts. We'd go away on camps when I was a member of the Cubs and later as a member of the Scouts. I can sleep through anything, as was proved when some of the older members of the scouts when I was a cub, including my cousin Ronny Turner, took me from my tent and dumped me next to the bonfire. They threw penny-bungers and double-bungers into the flames. I slept through all the loud explosions. Not impressed, the older scouts took me back into the tent and let me continue my peaceful sleep.

One time, when I was a member of the scouts, we were at a camp somewhere, and because it was raining, our box of matches was wet. We couldn't make a fire to cook the meat, so we ended up eating it raw. When you're young, you can eat anything, I guess.

Boy Scouts camp 1960 with Chris Hancock, me, and Helmet Mouldners

When I was a scout, the scouting association built a new scout hall in Hornsby. My dad asked me to pose as Mowgli, who was fighting the antagonist tiger, Shere Khan, for a painting on the wall of the new scout hall. The artist painting the wall wasn't impressed by how I was holding the knife, so he showed me how to do it properly and then got on with the painting. I was impressed by the finished artwork and was proud to have done it. Thanks, Dad!

In 1960-61, I went to the Boy Scouts Jamboree in Sydney. It was a successful jamboree with thousands of people attending, and I met a new friend there, a member of the Woolgoolga scout group.

With friend Greg at the 1960-61 Boy Scouts Jamboree

Greg and I became good friends. I went for a holiday at his place in Coffs Harbour a short time after the jamboree. His dad was a banana grower, and I learned a lot about growing bananas while I was there.

Greg even had a pet magpie, Maggie, who would help him polish his shoes!

Mum and Dad's Family History

A woman in England has traced the Nurthen family history back to the 15th Century and is still working on the project.

Our family once owned the property Piccadilly Circus in London. I have no idea when they owned the famous piece of land, but it is now a road junction and public space in London's West End in the city of Westminster.

The picture below is the Nurthen Coat of Arms.

There were two Nurthen families living in England. The first Nurthen family was the manufacturer of the fine silk cloth Kerseymere. The second Nurthen family, the Ernest Kersey Nurthen family (my family), used to sell Kerseymere via small boats along the coast of England and even over the channel, sometimes to the French coastal dwellers. The manufacturing Nurthen's emigrated to Australia in 1840, with my family following in 1860. My paternal great-grandfather, Mr. Thomas Kersey Nurthen, emigrated to Australia as a young boy with his parents and settled in Paddington, later becoming a master builder. He was an alderman of Paddington Council from 1902-1903 and was also chief of the Paddington Volunteer Fire Brigade. He was a Freemason for more than half a Century. He was married to Caroline Isabella Roberts (a relation of the famous painter Tom Roberts.)

My paternal great-grandfather and his wife at the silver anniversary of their marriage

A prominent resident of the Eastern Suburbs, he died at their home aged 87.

The middle names, Ernest Kersey, were related to our trade of selling Kerseymere. The middle names mean "honest traders of Kerseymere."

Thomas and Caroline had four boys and three girls. Thomas and his wife Caroline were also actors in the Woollahra Amateur Theatre Company. Thomas and Caroline played major roles in many of the productions the theatre company staged. My paternal grandfather Tom E K Nurthen, one of Thomas's boys, and his wife Maud (nee Le Boussiere) had three boys and two girls. The oldest of which, Walter Ernest Kersey Nurthen, was my father. Wal was the oldest of the five children, with the eldest sister Bell, born in 1913, and his two brothers John and Eric, with Joy, the last born child of the couple.

Dad died in May 1980 from Pageants Disease. As an electrician in the Air Force, Dad also taught flight crews how to use radar. The radar machines produced a lot of invisible electromagnetic radiation. It was this fact that caused Dad's death when he was only 69 years old.

Mona Nurthen

Walter and his wife Mona married in 1938. Wal and Mona (nee Kennedy) had two children. Alan was born on 6 July 1949, and my sister Sue was born on 5 May 1952. As I've said before, Wal and Mona were truly outstanding parents, both of whom went through the Great Depression and the Second World War. They had to put up with two kids who were born into the greatest time of history, the 60s and the 70s. But put up with us; they did, through all the "pain" that two "hippies" could bring to their lives.

My Mum, Mona, had a completely different upbringing. Her father died when he was 37 years old through alcohol abuse. After the death of her husband, Mrs. Kennedy found that she couldn't raise her daughter without an income, and Mona was adopted by her aunt and raised along with her cousin Dulcie Turner.

Mrs. Kennedy

Mum and Dad were friends with everybody they met, no matter what nationality their friends had. But Mum had an overwhelming hatred of the Japanese due to the fact that the Japs had murdered her brother, who was captured by the Japanese in New Guinea during the terrible fight to the death on the Kokada Trail. It was just a deep feeling that Dad agreed with due to the pain it caused Mum. Needless to say, no Japanese were their friends due to this event.

Mum died on 21st December 1992 from breast cancer. She was 81 years old. Mum was a great funds raiser for the Hornsby Hospital. I remember a week or so before Mum died, I was brushing her hair, and she told me where I could find her will and her bankbooks, etc. She was in a good state of mind, and we laughed a bit. But in the final days of her life, she was on morphine to kill the pain. Luckily, Christine, Tusyan, Bianca, Tianjin, and I were with Mum when she took her last breath. Even though her body was ruined by breast cancer, her pale blue eyes were in good order. She was an organ donor and donated her eyes to the hospital to help other people regain their sight.

When Mum died, the nurses asked us to leave the room for a couple of minutes, and when we were invited back in, the nurses had laid flowers all around her head on the pillow. It was the nurse's way of saying thank you for everything Mum had done for the hospital.

Mum was the only patient in the room, and her bed was close

to the window. Not long after Mum died, a strange-looking bird appeared at the window and started tapping hard on the glass. I believed it was Dad in bird form, coming to welcome her to join him. Luckily, the school was on summer holidays because I was so upset and drained by Mum's death that I spent a week sleeping on the couch. I hardly ate anything and was severely depressed by her passing. Luckily, less than two weeks after Mum died, Brennan turned up for a long holiday with us. The first time he'd been to Australia since Tereza took him back to South Africa in 1977. Brennan's arrival turned the tide of my depression, and I started to feel happy again. But it was such a pity that Mum died before Brennan arrived here as she was so looking forward to seeing him again.

Vera

I've been with my woman Vera for almost 27 wonderful years. I'm her third long-term relationship, and she is my third long-term relationship. You'd be hard to find a woman with more love for her man than her. I met her on a blind date, and when I first saw her, it was love at first sight. Vera is staunchly monogamous, loyal to her man, and with a great sense of humour. But don't cross her! If you do, you've made an enemy for life.

As a young woman, Vera was a reserve member of the Russian Special Air Service (SAS.) She was trained to kill with her bare hands and any weapon she could get her hands on. She made 1300 parachute jumps with the SAS but stopped when another reserve member of the SAS was killed when jumping with her. He made a fatal mistake – he didn't pack his own parachute before he jumped.

Before Vera and I finally moved in together, she lived at Cherrybrook in a townhouse with her son Victor and daughter Ksenia.

One day, a young thug turned up with seven of his rough and tough mates. When Vera answered the front door, the man said he wanted to speak with his former girlfriend, who was sitting in the backyard with Victor and some of his friends. When Vera let the man in, he then proceeded to get into an argument with his old girlfriend and then started to drag her through the house by her hair. Vera stopped him and told him to leave the house. When he got to the front door, all of his mates were standing there waiting for him. He exited the door and then turned and threw a punch at Vera. Vera stepped back, punched him in the face, and broke his nose. He screamed, and then the rest of the thugs lined up - one at a time in the narrow doorway - and had a go at her. She took them all out one by one. The end result of the fight was the thugs received 9 broken fingers and 4 broken noses without them laying a hand on Vera. The last young man in line at the door panicked, turned and ran. Vera chased him down the driveway, grabbed him by his trackie pants, lifted him off the ground, and said: 'If you don't get off my property, you die here!' She dropped him to the ground, and he ran down the driveway holding up his pants to cover his bare arse. In a few minutes, three cop cars blocked the street outside. The police started to arrest all of the thugs, many of whom were in serious pain after the fight and willingly gave up to the police. They were all taken to Hornsby Hospital for treatment and then charged with assault.

No one laid a hand on Vera, but she was completely puffed out and breathing hard after the fight.

One of the female police officers was in absolute awe of Vera and her fighting abilities. She said to Vera: 'We could really use you up at The Cross on weekends.' Vera's response: 'I only look after my family.' That's Vera. A true legend!

When Vera first arrived in Australia, she barely knew the English language. Ksenia and Victor were fine, though, and could speak the language clearly and effectively. Vera and I used to communicate via a Russian-Australian dictionary until she learned the language well enough. Vera's lack of English was a real hoot at first. One time, we were at the Glebe markets, and Vera, while studying some of the hand-crafted items for sale, said to me: 'Do you like a good hand job?' The people around us started to giggle, and I said to Vera: 'Yes. But not here, okay.'

Another time in the supermarket, she said to a young lad stacking the shelves: 'Please can you help me? My pussy is hungry, and I need to feed it.' The young guy almost had a heart attack! Ha ha.

In June 2001, I was involved in a car accident. It was the second car accident I'd been involved in for 3 months. Neither of the accidents was my fault. Both of my cars were written off. In the first car accident, I was almost pushed under the back of a two-ton truck by the car following me. The woman behind me was on her way to a wedding and was more concerned with putting on her makeup in the rearview mirror instead of keeping an eye on the road. When her car pushed me into the back of the truck, I took it out of my windscreen and came within a few centimeters of my face. Other than a couple of small abrasions and a cracked tooth, I was fine. Then the cop who turned up was more intent on cracking on to the woman who rammed me! I couldn't believe it.

In the second car accident, 3 months after the first, I was clubbed pretty badly. Vera was living in her townhouse at Cherrybrook, and I was living in Mona Vale. It was completely different in Cherrybrook. There were trees that didn't grow on the beaches, and vice versa. It was a great getaway, and I'd go up there every weekend when I finished working at the studio. Anyway, in the second accident, a young female P plater took the bottom corner of Killeaton Street, coming out of the S-bends way too fast. She lost control of the car, and it started weaving its way toward the oncoming traffic. Everyone saw it coming, and cars were turning around or heading up driveways. When I saw the car speeding toward me, I knew it was going to hit me. I turned up the nearest driveway – and the metal gates were locked. I looked to my right and saw the car in the air and heading straight for me! Then she crashed, still in the air, into the driver's side of my car. I was pushed 3 meters sideways into a tree. I was covered in broken glass. My driver's side window had fallen into my lap in perfect shape. The glass that hit me was from the Holden sedan. After the car hit me, it bounced back a few feet and became suspended on the meter-high grass and dirt verge, teetering back and forth like a seesaw. I tried to get out of my car. The tree was jamming the passenger side door, and my door was smashed, so I climbed out the window. I went to stand up and fell onto the pavement. Something was wrong with my right leg, so I crawled to the other car. I really wanted to beat the shit out of the other driver. Two accidents in 3 months! Come on! I was halfway there, crawling like a baby, when the woman emerged from the other car. She was an Asian girl of 17. I stopped and sat up as best I could. Then, an Indian man who lived over the road brought me a cup of coffee. Half the street was outside with the noise of the crashing cars. A neighbour had rung the police and the ambulance. I rang Vera and told her what happened. When the ambulance got there not long after, along with the police, a policeman asked an ambulance attendant: "Where are the bodies from the beamer?" The ambo told him that I was sitting in the back of the ambulance. The cop looked at me and couldn't believe it. He expected a couple of deceased people, and I looked relatively okay. Vera turned up and asked if I wanted to go to the hospital, and I said no, I'd be okay. Then the owner of the car, the woman's Dad, turned up and tried to convince the police that her tyre had blown out and that was why she had lost control of the car. The police didn't believe him and charged her with dangerous driving and cancelled her license on the spot.

Vera then drove me back to her place, and in the bathroom, I undressed, shook all of the glass from my body, and climbed into a warm bath. There was glass everywhere! I was wearing a T-shirt, a jumper and a leather jacket. There was glass inside all of my clothing, my undies, and even my socks and shoes!

Not long after, my right collarbone started to hurt, and my right knee was playing up, so I approached the NRMA and saw a doctor. He represented the car that hit me under their insurance. He tried to brush it all aside and said he could arrange for an operation for my shoulder blade to be straightened. *No thanks.* It involved shearing down the top of the bone. It would grow back to its original shape in 18 months or so. I selected to receive acupuncture and muscle massage for about a year.

Then, the bad news: I HAD TO GIVE UP SURFING! The naturopath said because of the damage to my right knee, if I kept on surfing, then I'd be on a walking stick within 18 months. He advised that I take up body boarding as it would give my legs exercise by paddling, wearing flippers, and strengthening my shoulder and collar bone. I took his advice, and 23 years later, I'm nowhere near having a walking stick.

In 2008, Vera and I booked a fly-drive holiday to Cairns. From Cairns, we drove up to Port Douglas and stayed there for 10 days. We took a drive one day into the mountains behind Cairns and went to a place called Mareeba. We went to a coffee manufacturing business. You could try all the different coffees they made, and there were plastic cups in which you could collect chocolates, which were supplied by the coffee company. Being a chocolate freak, I filled three cups. I also filled my pockets and had chocolate to munch on for days. Hey, like I said, I'm a chocolate freak – *big time!* I had to have some extra chocolates to munch on ... Aaah ... heaven!

Vera has a strong connection with the Russians living in Australia. She does this through her and her daughter Ksenia, who runs the non-profit business, The Russian Culture Center, based next to my acting studio in Brookvale. Thanks to Vera's clout in the Russian community, we were invited to attend the Russian Embassy in Woollahra for an event: it was the celebration of Yuri Gagarin's first trip into space as the sole person in the capsule, the Vostok 1 in 1961. It was the only space trip he made. He died in a MIG-15 with his pilot Vladimir Seryogin on March 27, 1968. After the flight into space, he became a global celebrity touring widely to promote Russian achievements. Gagarin is buried in the Laid-to-Rest Wall of the Kremlin on Red Square.

With Alexi at the Russian Embassy, 2021

There was also a man at the party, Alexi, who had been a trainer to the cosmonauts. He was very old, and his English basically didn't exist, but his daughter spoke the language well. We talked for an hour or more, and she told me the full story of what her father had done. In 1965, Alexi was also the flight trainer for Alexei Arkhipovich, the first man to walk in space.

Very interesting life Alexi lived, and it was wonderful to hear the full story.

Early teens and school life

Hopefully, everyone has a few close friends. My parents, along with those raising me, were also my closest friends. My closest friend was my mother. My second closest friend was my father. (He put in the boot. Ouch!)

I had a good time at school. I was always one of the leaders. When I moved from primary classes to high school in 1962, I tried all of the available sports. But they eventually bored me, and by 1965, the only sport I was interested in was surfing. Luckily, my friend Andrew Deacon was repeating a year and had his driver's license. So, on sports days, on Wednesday afternoons, Andrew and I would use his mother's car to get us to the beach.

There wasn't a problem with this arrangement at school because my mother was heavily involved with a lot of the school's activities, and when I asked Mum to approach the deputy headmaster, she agreed. The deputy headmaster said that would be fine, except anything that took part out of school meant that Andrew and I weren't insured under the school's policy. Not a problem! We were probably the first surfers in NSW school history to take advantage of going surfing on sports days. When my daughters Bianca and Tianjin were in high school, surfing was part of the sports curriculum, and both my girls took it up. So, I guess I paved the way for them.

There were no predator teachers at my high school. The men and women who taught us were the best teachers. They cared about what they did. This didn't make me a good student, though. I passed 4 out of 6 classes for the Year 10 exams, my final year at school. I passed history, tech drawing, English, and Maths (with a lot of help from the head Maths teacher - who lived down the road from me - every couple of afternoons after school each week.) I passed all my exams at the ordinary level, with a credit in English. I failed French and science. But as an adult, I find science very interesting and informative.

Year 4 rugby team. Me, second from the right in the back row.

In the above photo is our under-8 stone rugby team. The only problem was that all of the other teams, except Normanhurst, had players weighing well over 8 stone, mostly from the private schools, who took no notice of the weight restriction. The elite sort of people who felt empowered by the private school setup. They felt superior to us public school boys. That didn't bother us, though, as we took our revenge on the private school boys when we travelled by train to sporting events. We'd harass them and kick their bags out of the train. No one messes with us, particularly elitist private school students! I guess we were just trying to show them that we were, in fact, their equal and wouldn't take any shit from them.

Late teens and young adult life

When I was 17, one of my friends was Allan Coleman. We met through surfing. We nicknamed Allan Yo-Yo. When he surfed, his front hand would go up and down, up and down, like he was playing with a yo-yo.

He was the first person we knew who'd been to jail over the non-productive, harmful *War on Drugs* program. From what I heard, he died around 1990, still addicted to heroin. I think he had AIDS by then, too, probably through dirty needles.

What a waste of time with police abuse towards addicts. *Lock em up. No questions*, when by now, in many countries, drugs are more accessible. Drug addicts should be treated medically, not as criminals.

When I was 19, my Dad and Mr. Watson, who lived below our house in the valley, helped us; well they did all the work, thank goodness. My Dad and Mr. Watson were good with cars. The old Austin A40 panel van they fitted out for us, we drove all the way from Hornsby to Noosa Heads and back again.

On the trip, it was me, Yo-Yo, and Glenn.

Glenn didn't surf, but he was a good critic whether you had a bad day or a good day.

But even back then, Yo-Yo had an addiction: pills. He kept

them in our food box.

Glenn and I decided to get him off the pills, so we trashed them. He wasn't happy when he found out. But Yo-Yo was a great guy. He was a lot of fun. Good to hang out with. Never reverted to payback or anything like it. He had a good feeling for life.

In early 1968, I tried some white pills that Yo-Yo had given me when we were surfing at Kiddies Corner in Palm Beach. It made everything feel out of joint. Not connected to what you should be feeling. Surfing was useless under those circumstances - I couldn't feel my feet on the board. No sensation. No feelings of anything. It was like I couldn't win ... so we gave it up. It was just the drugs we took to give that sensation of not being connected.

Good lesson, though: Be straight when you go surfing. It's the only way to get organic pleasure while surfing a wave.

Vale Allan/Yo-Yo. It's a pity we lost you.

Yo, 1968

Then, in 1970, I changed to another group of surfers. This new group included the Wog - because with his crazy black hair, he looked like a Gollywog. And Goliath, well, because he was 6 foot two inches in height. There were other surfers who we'd hook up with as well. Good times.

And that year, I was heading overseas! I was stoked!

Goliath and Wog at Byron Bay lighthouse

They were different times back then. The war in Vietnam and other political problems were bothering the young and some of the older people as well. Marches, demonstrations, exciting times.

I was involved in the draft for Vietnam, but my number never came up. My Dad would have fought to keep me out of the army. Luckily, he never had to. So I was free to go! … Which I did at a rapid speed.

Dad's work

After my Dad had settled in after the Second World War, he got a job in the NSW Railways department. He put the skills he learned in the RAAF as a sergeant electrician to apply for the head job.

When the weather was fine, it was easygoing at the Hornsby signal box. Dad and the other guys liked to play around. They always enjoyed giving you a jolt from the electric shock points downstairs at the entry-level to the signal box. They would tell you, 'Don't be afraid to touch the two points; it won't hurt you.' Yeah right. You always received a jolt, which was harmless, but you certainly felt it!

The signal box itself was on the second floor, where the guys changing the electrical points on the train tracks could clearly see what they were doing. Everyone took a break upstairs. As I said, they could have fun with you.

But, if the weather was filthy, Dad could be called out at any hour to fix broken down train signals or other electrical problems. He was responsible for the railway tracks from Hornsby to the Hawkesbury River.

Dad would be woken at 2 or 3 in the early morning hours. He had to be out there fixing the problems.

Big responsible job.

Sometimes, he worked in the signals box at Pennant Hills station. Looking after the tracks between Pennant Hills and Hornsby.

Dad worked that job until he retired at age 65.

Now it's 67. Thanks government!

Dad was my eldest son, Brennan's paternal grandfather.

Whenever Tereza and I had to go out somewhere, we knew that Brennan was in good hands. Plus, Mum was there to help out. Brennan loved helping Dad feed his exotic bird collection, from tiny finches to brightly coloured peacocks.

Dad was a good grandpa. He gave Brennan the opportunity to grow and explore things.

Brennan's 3rd birthday with Dad and some of his friends. Blowing out the candles.

The picture below features my Dad, his brothers John and Eric, and their sister Joy, along with their Mum Maud, at a picnic in Avalon Beach in 1961. Bell wasn't in the photo as she was already running the sheep station with her husband, Bob.

Dad, John, and Eric with their younger sister Joy and their mother Maud (my paternal grandmother)

Maud lived a long life, and whenever I visited her in the old folk's home where she lived in Waitara, she always had the same question just after I kissed her. 'Have you been smoking cigarettes?' Me: 'Yes, I have grandma.' Maud: 'You've been a naughty boy' and then cuffed me on the arm and laughed.

Maud had a bright outlook on life.

Alan Nurthen

Some extra details on my travels to South Africa

1971 to 1975

All at Sea

Back in the days when ships were ships and not the modern floating hotels that they are today. When a trip to South Africa costs $240, including everything on board in your ticket, 3 meals a day, and all entertainment, less anything you bought from the purser's office, like duty-free cigarettes or alcohol, it took 16 days to get from Sydney to Durban, with stops in Melbourne, Adelaide, and Freemantle and then the long voyage across the Indian ocean.

When ships were ships. The P&O Orsova

Being a surfer, I spent a lot of time in the swimming pool and even entered some of the pool events, winning every event I participated in. Most of the travelers were British people returning home for a visit, and none of them knew the ocean, so it wasn't hard to win the pool events. One of the hardest things to do was to jump in with a boiler suit on, swim to the end of the pool, take off the suit, and then place it at the end of the pool. The hard part was placing the boiler suit on the deck, which was extremely heavy when wet, but I somehow managed to do it and won that event as well. It was then that one of the P&O officers approached me and said: 'Can you stay out of the pool for a while and give the other passengers a go.' 'Oh sure, not a problem,' I agreed, embarrassed, realizing that I'd won every event I'd entered. Such was life at sea for the first time passengers from Australia. There were movies to see on board and other indoor events as well.

I made a voyage on the P&O ship Orsova to Durban on my first visit overseas, staying for 5 months in South Africa. Later in my travels that year, I flew home from Europe and back to Australia.

Paso and a confused Madrid taxi driver

While we were in Spain, a taxi driver was puzzled over our surfboard bags. I showed him a photo of waves I had cut from a surfing magazine, but he still didn't get it. Paso and I couldn't speak Spanish, so hand gestures were essential, but they didn't work either. Madrid is a long way from the ocean, and the man couldn't figure out what was in the travel bags. In 1971, no one living in Madrid was a surfer, and the taxi driver most likely had never seen the ocean. You had to live in San Sebastian or somewhere else on the coast to be a surfer.

Before I went back to South Africa in early 1972, I returned to my trade, lithography, for the first time in my life. I was the night printer at a printing factory in the inner city. I had two men laboring on the machine, and I looked after the printing. We were printing a magazine called *Ribald*. It had sexy photos of scantily dressed women along with racy stories by the editors - or people sending stories to them. Late at night, old men in raincoats or overcoats would turn up and gather up the miss-printed magazines, put the magazines in a shopping trolley, and go off. I think they were selling them on the streets for next to nothing.

I told Mum and Dad that I was printing Ribald magazine. And after that, if Dad was ever asked what I was doing, he'd say: 'Alan's printing art books.' Go, Dad!

Then later, in June 1972, I made another round trip to Africa on the P&O ship Oriana. After flying to Durban in 1975 to marry Tereza, I also came home on an Italian ship with Tereza and Brennan. You can see amazing sights from the deck of a ship, whales broaching at sea, with nothing around you but an endless array of oceans.

And my favourite sight at sea was lounging at the stern of the ship to observe kitchen hands throwing big cricket-sized bags of leftover food overboard - which were attacked by hungry sharks who followed the ships across the Indian ocean with the huge sharks picking up another ship on the return back to Australia. You would not want to fall overboard!

Speaking of which, on the Italian ship Tereza, Brennan, and I were travelling to Australia on, the ship stopped in the middle of the Indian Ocean next to another cruise ship where a passenger, drunk and showing off, fell from the ship railing into the sea. As he was walking along the railing, the ship lurched in the swell, and the man fell overboard. We had a good look for him along with the other ship, but it was fruitless as the man had either fallen under the ship and torn apart by the propellers or eaten by the scavenging sharks.

On my second voyage back to Durban in 1972, we ran into a horrendous storm in The Great Australian Bight. I was standing in the topmost part of the ship with my mate Tom Thompson (who I met on my first trip to Durban and was returning home after spending time with my parents and me) and a South African surfer, who was also returning home. We were surfing the huge waves with the ship and hanging on tightly to a railing when suddenly, the entire front of the ship went completely underwater, and it felt like the ship was taking a one-way trip to the bottom of the ocean. All we could see in front of us was salt water, which covered the whole front of the ship completely. The ship shuddered and groaned and eventually popped out the other side of the swell. What was a fun "surfing" experience turned truly frightening, and we were glad to be alive!

The positive thing about rough seas was that they were handy, as most passengers who were seasick took to their cabins. That meant at meal times, you could order whatever you wanted, for there was so much food left over. And this was an English ship with excellent food. I remember one time that I ordered three main meals and had seven dessert dishes. Heaven for a hungry young boy!

In fact, the only time I ever felt seasick was on the English Channel ferry when we crossed from France to England, and the English Channel was rough with wind-ripped waves. I was doing fine until I went to the toilet. It stank of vomit from the other passengers, and I came so close to throwing up with the horrible smell.

Fancy Dress party with my cabin mates

On my second voyage back to Australia on the Shaw Savill

liner Ocean Monarch, late in 1972, I was entrusted by Tom Thompson to look after his hi-fi equipment that I was delivering to my sister and her husband courtesy of Tom. In wild seas off The Great Australian Bight, I ventured down to the hold to check on the hi-fi gear. I was halfway down the long ladder into the hold when the ship lurched violently, and I found myself parallel to the hold floor. I hung on like crazy until the ship rolled the other way, slamming me back into the ladder, where I descended as fast as I could. When I got to the bottom of the ladder, a crew member was stunned. He couldn't believe I'd made it down below in one piece. Once I'd checked that the hi-fi gear was in good shape, the crew member told me he'd tell me when to ascend the ladder. When he gave me the nod, I scaled the ladder like a water rat and made it safely back up. Now, that was an adventure, to say the least! Plus, Tom's hi-fi gear in the hold was being well looked after.

Me and Tom at my parent's house in 1975

Tom also lived a long and fruitful life. He died at the age of 92 years. For a few years before I met Tom, he was one of the photographers for numerous surfing magazines. Tom was an instrument baby, and his right arm and his right leg were crippled. He could hobble fast enough, and he always stayed up with you, no matter his affliction. Tom couldn't surf, so he took up surfing photography. He moved to Thailand after being attacked in the street by three African women in Durban. This was the last straw for Tom in South Africa, and he moved to Thailand, where he taught English to the locals and lived a quiet life. I visited Tom in Thailand with two of my kids, Tush and Bianca, in 1996. It's a real shame as I never got back there again to see him after the 1996 holiday.

I'd been to Thailand before - when returning home from my first trip overseas in 1971. But it was under different circumstances. The war in Vietnam was raging, and Bangkok was full of American soldiers. The airport was packed with American warplanes of every description. It's not a good place to be - especially with my long hair and my pink jeans.

In 1996, when I returned with the kids, we stayed next to Tom's cabin at the Cool Breeze Bungalows at Kata Beach. Tom was a good babysitter, so I could go out at night with my friend Bob, who I met on the Air New Zealand flight to Thailand.

Bob was living in New Zealand by then, but he was Canadian by birth and played music in Canada and America before he moved to New Zealand. When we got to know each other on the flight over, I nicknamed him Banjo Bob. He had played banjo in Joan Baez's band at the Newport Folk Festival in the early sixties.

Banjo was flying to Phuket Island by plane. The kids and I were booked on a bus. On the way down on the bus, we were pulled over by a police patrol checkpoint. The police searched the bus and found that one of the people who worked on the bus was down in the bag hold. He was searching through the bags for valuables. The police arrested him, and we went on our way.

Luckily, he didn't get to our bags by the time he was caught.

Banjo and I got up to all sorts of trouble, travelling around on our trail bikes, dropping into bars, and talking to all sorts of people. There were a lot of ladyboys living on Phuket Island. In a way, they seemed more ladylike than the real thing. I made a few friends with the ladyboys. Their English was good, and they were fun to drink with.

Despite what happened on the bus on the way down to Phuket, Thais were basically honest people. There was a bar next door to where we were living. It was run by the bar manager, Kaew Saenbutdee, a lady boy. I became good friends with Kaew.

A couple of times, she looked after the kids. We had our

passports, some Thai money, and a few other valuables sitting around, and nothing was ever touched or moved.

Around that time, Banjo and I went to an open-air bar somewhere up the coast. All the bars were playing really loud music. Music of all styles. It took me a while to get used to it. It was deafening!

I ended up playing pool with some Thai guys. One of them, setting up a shot, exposed a gun in a holster at his waist. He saw me notice it. He said he was a detective and that if we had any trouble, we should call him. He gave me his card.

When we were leaving the bar, this rabid dog – with missing fur, scars all over him, and one workable eye - attacked me when I started my motorbike. I kicked him off so he wouldn't bite me, and he came back again. *Hard.* This dog was really vicious! I gave him a really big kick, and he shot off into the bush. No way did I want rabies or anything sinister like that. I rode off out of there - *fast!* Before the dog ran from the scrub and had a go at me – again!

The Thais have a conflicted view of dogs. Something I found out later.

Some of the Thais treat them as part of the family, while others see dogs as bad spirits.

We got around on a trail bike while we were there, and I used to run the kids around on the back of the bike while checking out the sights. I'd take Tush somewhere and then pick up Bianca and take her to Tush. It worked well for us.

Going for a ride with Bianca

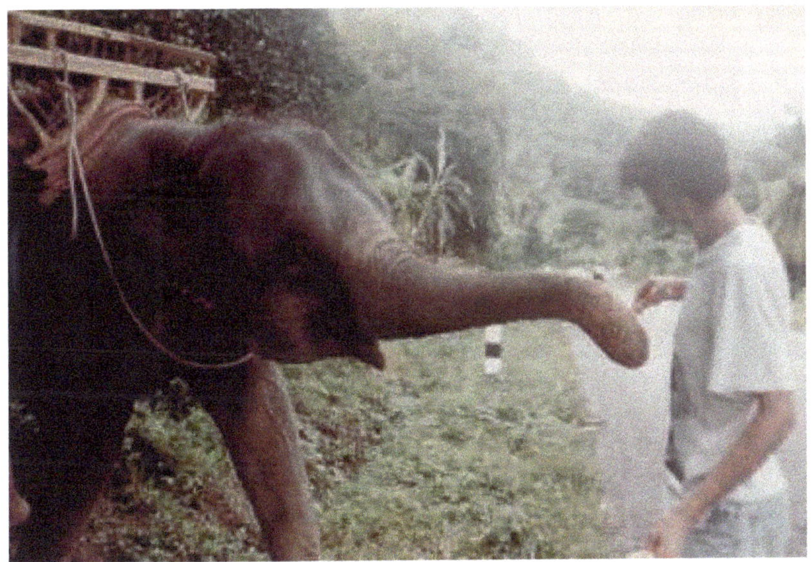

Tush feeding bananas to a hungry elephant

Tush stayed at our cabin one day, so I took Bianca shopping at the south end of the island. She wanted to buy some gifts for her friends, and there was a good shop there. Near where we parked the bike, there was a sit-down-and-chill-out area with a meter-high brick wall surrounding it with a cutout door and a roof overhead. When we were getting off the bike, Bianca noticed a man in the shed beating a dog with a piece of wood. We could only see the dog when it tried to escape. Bianca was horrified. She said: 'Dad! *Do something!'* I ran over and told the man to stop hitting the dog. I couldn't speak Thai, but he got my drift. He gave me a filthy look. He waited till I walked away and then went back to beating the dog.

I told Bianca to go into the shop, which she did.

I then approached the man again and had a go at him. He didn't give a shit. I gave up and joined Bianca in the shop. Bianca told the woman running the shop that she'd have to carry the presents all the way home, so the store owner wrapped the gifts extremely well. They were mobiles made with hanging sea shells. Extremely fragile. We bought a strong paper bag while in the shop, and Bianca packed the presents, wrapped in pop wrap by the shop's owner, into the bag. To her credit, Bianca carried the gifts in her lap on the bus back to Bangkok and in her lap again while flying back home. The presents were made in tip-top order and then distributed to her friends.

When we came out of the shop, Bianca said: 'Dad, go and check on the dog.' I went over to the shed and saw the dog lying on the floor, covered in blood. He was dead, without a doubt. I knew Bianca couldn't see what I saw. I said: 'The dogs are gone.' It was a lie, but it worked. Relieved, she hopped onto the bike, and off we went.

I didn't understand then about the conflicting emotions that Thai's have over dogs. If I had known this back then, would I have handled it differently? Probably not. I don't like cruelty to animals. I would have definitely tried to stop the man.

Not long after we arrived, I was riding around on my bike

one night when a woman running a bar called me over. I had a few drinks with her, and we hit it off. When she suggested we should make love, I was *in,* like Errol Flynn! While we were slowly getting into it, I put my hand around to the front of her body and – *Shock! Horror!* "She" had a penis! My hard-on disappeared immediately.

I made some excuses, but she laughed about it, so I relaxed, and we had another drink. When I left, she called out: 'Come back soon!'

After the incident with the ladyboy, Tom explained how to spot them. Tom said if they had an Adam's Apple, they were men and not girls. Most of the ladyboys had good jobs as they were saving up for a sex change operation. The information Tom gave me was very useful - and saved me from further embarrassment! On a brighter note, while we were there, a young Thai guy fell in love with Bianca and gave her a nice necklace. It was cute to watch. He was a good kid.

With Tom and Banjo leaving for Bangkok and the flight home

When we left Thailand and arrived at the airport, there was a big sign on the wall saying, "Welcome New Zealand Airline passengers." Our plane had been delayed in New Zealand, and the airline staff had laid out a spread for us. Nice of them. But then Tush and Bianca had a scary thought: 'We were stranded at the airport!' I'd been in this situation once before on a flight back to Australia from Africa. I knew we'd be well looked after. After dinner, we crossed over the super-busy road below us on the overhead passage to the airport hotel. A nice room was arranged for us. Once we settled into the room, we went downstairs and sat in a booth with a TV set. There was a black and white Charlie Chaplin film on the screen. The kids couldn't work out why it was in black and white and didn't have a soundtrack. I explained it to them, and they slowly got into it. In the end, they liked it.

When we were heading back to our room, I was walking behind the kids and noticed that Bianca's white trousers had blood on them. She was having her first period. When we got to the room, I told her what was happening. She was fourteen, and it frightened her at first. I calmed her down and ordered some sanitary pads from the front desk.

Then, the next day at the airport, I discovered that we'd have to pay an extra "leaving charge" to get on the plane. We'd spent the last of our money and had nothing left. Luckily, a Canadian couple in the queue behind us paid the fee for us.

Alan Nurthen

My first trip to South Africa

When hitching to Cape Town and then back to Durban on my first trip to South Africa in 1971, Paso and I ended up in a small town with a few shops and a police station. If you were young and white and on the road, the police would let you stay at the police station. They'd put you in a black policeman's office. It was always nice and warm in the office. You'd lay your sleeping bags on the floor and have a good night's sleep. Then, in the morning, they'd bring you a cup of coffee, and you were free to go and find some breakfast somewhere and then hit the road again.

One time, Paso and I were not that sleepy and decided to put together a fingerprint card. I'd place my thumb onto the card, then Paso would place his index finger on the card, and so it went until the card was filled. We'd write a phony name on the card and a description of the criminal.

We had a lot of fun doing it – and best of luck finding that guy!

On that same trip, we ended up in a small town, but there was nowhere to sleep. No local police station, either. But there was a public phone box outside a small supermarket. So we wandered around the back of the supermarket to the rubbish bins and picked up a few cardboard cartons. We then flattened the boxes and laid some on the floor of the public phone box to keep the cold from our backsides. We laid the rest against the side of the phone box to give us some privacy. It looked fine, so we settled down and eventually went to sleep.

When we woke up the next morning, there were these Africans standing outside the phone box, just staring at us. They couldn't believe it; here were two young white guys sleeping in a phone box! In racist South Africa! What are these white guys doing in a phone box?!? It was obviously what they were thinking. But not speaking their dialect, I couldn't tell them what we were doing.

Back in Durban, at the Dolphin Hotel, we always left the rear windows open when we were glassing surfboards. The windows, two stories up, looked over an alleyway, and on the other side of the alley was a grog shop for the Africans. One day, we heard a racket and went to the window to see what was happening. An old African man sitting on a fold-up chair was abusing his wife. The wife took it for a little while and then grabbed the chair the old man was sitting on and proceeded to bash him senselessly. We couldn't believe it and shouted our support for the old woman.

When I was making surfboards at the Dolphin Hotel, I paid Wilson (who worked as a waiter at the hotel) far more than what the hotel was paying him to rough-shape surfboards for me. He was stoked to have another well-paying job to supplement his wages. We got on well, and I told him about Australia, but he couldn't relate to another country so far away and across a vast ocean. I don't think he actually understood what I was telling him.

With Wilson at the Dolphin Hotel.

Shaping a surfboard in the backyard of the Dolphin Hotel. 1971.

When I returned to South Africa in 1972, I moved into the Blenheim Hotel on Gillespie Street, one street back from the beachfront in Durban. I was living out the back of the hotel in the cabins. Around this time, my old friend Tom Thompson, who managed the Blenheim, asked if I'd like to take nine of the African staff up to Zululand to have their work passports stamped at the local police station. We took the hotel Kombi van with eight of the guys sitting in the open back and Phillip, the head waiter at the hotel, sitting up front with me.

Once we'd completed the job, one of the guys asked me if we could possibly visit his village so he could see his wife and his kids. So off we set across miles of dusty roads to the village. When we finally got to the village, a guard from the compound noticed me. He whipped out his machete from his belt and approached me. He was getting ready to swipe me with the machete! Luckily, Phillip, the head waiter, saw what was happening and approached the guard.

He told him that I was regarded by the Africans he knew as a Prince: someone who cared about people from all different races and creeds. This calmed the guard down, and he let me enter with the others.

We spent the whole afternoon there, and I played with the kids who lived there. Later, when it was getting late in the day, we said our goodbyes and left.

But I must say the village guards had a sexy life. With all the men working somewhere else and only the women and children in the village, the guards could have their pick of the wives. No one ever spoke about this, though. It was just the way they lived their lives.

When I returned to Durban, Tom and the owners of the hotel were relieved, to say the least. I should have been back earlier that day. They believed anything could have happened to me and the guys with me. I explained what happened, and they laughed and chewed me out a little, and then it was forgotten.

Back in Durban, the housemaids were always on the lookout for what they could steal from the travellers. If a maid liked one of your t-shirts, she would move it from where she found it and put it somewhere else in the room. When she came back the next day, if the T-shirt was in the same place she had left it, she'd move it again to a new place in the room. If it was still there the next day, she would steal it. I'd seen this happen to people before, so I kept a good eye on the few things I owned.

When I was in South Africa for the first time in 1971, I hung out with a couple of local surfers who surfed the Wedge at the West Street Pier. I was sitting on the grass at the top of the hill overlooking the Wedge when one of the local surfers, Dave Hebbler, was coming out of the surf. He came up the hill, and we said hi and chatted.

Dave's board was a dark green colour all over.

Now, here's the weird thing: when back in Australia, saving up for my second trip to South Africa, I had a dream one night not long before I left for overseas. In the dream, Dave exited the surfboard, and his surfboard was still dark green, but this time, it had two yellow triangles on the top and the bottom of the board.

So much for the strange dream, I thought. But on my second trip there in 1972, I surfed a few times with Dave, riding his fully green board before I left for a trip to Johannesburg. A few weeks later, when I returned from my trip, I saw Dave exiting the surf, but this time, it had a yellow triangular patch on the top and the bottom of the board. Just like in my dream! He'd snapped his board in half while I was away, and a local surfboard maker had repaired it. I couldn't believe it!

So, does this dream mean I could see the future? Maybe not, but that dream still bothers me to this day. It was like some weird sort of Deja vu.

In Durban, the Alley Brats also lived. They were a nasty bunch of people who hung out at the beach. None of them surfed, but the beach was a safe place to hang out as nobody bothered them there. The leader of the Alley Brats pushed himself around in a small cart as he'd lost his legs in a shoot-out with the cops. He was so badly wounded that his legs were amputated.

The Alley Brats made a big part of their living from raiding people's flats. They'd get a straight-looking girl to book an apartment, stay for a couple of days, and then pass a copy of the key to the Alley Brats. They'd keep an eye on the place, and when someone moved in, they'd use the key to break in and steal whatever they wanted.

When I was there in 1975 to marry Tereza, I was living with Tom Thompson in his flat. One day, I went for a surf, and as I was approaching the elevator on the eighth floor, the door opened, and three Alley Brats emerged from the lift. I didn't think much of it at the time, but when I got back from my surfing session, I saw the door open and found that they'd stolen all of my clothes and the suit that I bought for the wedding. And they'd taken all my clothes in my multi-colored round-barrel travel bag! The bastards!

I walked down the street to the Blenheim Hotel, and I told Tom what had happened. He said to contact the police. This I did, and a few days later, the police called in and asked me to accompany them to the police station as they'd found the thieves. When I got there, I didn't recognise any of the Alley Brats, as the police had worked them over extremely well. Their faces were so swollen that I couldn't recognise any of them.

The sad thing was that all of my clothes were given to the tailor they used for alterations, and he'd made them all smaller, so the clothes were useless. I had to call my Dad and ask him to send me some money so I could buy some new clothes.

Tereza's father, Bob James, Brennan's maternal grandfather, wasn't happy about me marrying his daughter, but his wife supported us. She could see it was true love between the two of us. Bob knew I wanted to return home to Australia, therefore taking Tereza and Brennan with me. He tried to keep me there by saying there were plenty of jobs, but I was involved in the surfing industry back home. It got so heavy at one point I thought he was planning to put me in a pair of concrete shoes and take me for a walk in Durban harbour. But old Bob truly loved Brennan and his daughter. He was a great "Boompa" and father. Strict, but fair.

Frog Races and Pink Jeans

Note my pink cord jeans in the above photo. The people I knew when walking the streets of South Africa recognised me straight away as I was the only person who wore pink jeans. They definitely stood out from the crowd!

When I returned to Durban on my second visit in 1972, a newspaper reporter came on board and took the above photo. The photo shows six Aussie surfers (me, third from the right) coming to South Africa chasing waves and a South African returning home.

So, who's the South African in the above photo? … Give up?

Look at everyone's feet. He's the only person wearing boots, and we all wear thongs.

Typical Australians!

On my first trip to South Africa, I spent a lot of time

hitchhiking around the country. I hitched from Durban to Cape Town and back again, a round trip of 6500 kilometers. I made these trips with my flatmate Paso, a guy I met from Melbourne, not long after I arrived in the country.

You could spend a lot of time waiting for cars when out on the highway, and we used to walk ahead on the road to kill time while waiting for a lift. I cut a piece of cardboard from a box before the trip to Cape Town, and I wrote in black text *Aussies to Cape Town* on one side and *Aussies to Durban* on the other side. This sign got us all the way there and back. Ah, the beauty of a simple sign!

Paso with our handmade sign.

When we scored a ride, I'd sit in the front with the driver. I enjoyed having a chat. Paso sat in the back and took in the scenery, as he wasn't in the habit of talking to strangers. Paso was a big guy, and he was good as protection if we ever needed it. But we never had an incident while hitching. The only problem was just one time. And we caused it through fear of a sudden death. We were in the back of a utility with an Afrikaner and his wife sitting up front. Every now and then, the old woman would tap on the rear window and point out something interesting to look at. We were driving along the coastal highway with fantastic views of the ocean and the surrounding areas when, all of a sudden, the utility veered off the road and headed straight for the cliff above the ocean! The car was about to go over the edge of the cliff! Paso and I thought that the old guy had a heart attack and lost control of the car. We quickly threw our bags and ourselves out the back of the utility and rolled along in the dirt. The utility stopped short of the cliff, and the woman got out and said: "Hey man, we were stopping to show you the view!" Yes, it's very embarrassing. They ended up dropping us off in the middle of nowhere when they turned off to their farm. It was a long way to the next town, and it took ages until a car came by, which luckily stopped for us. Our sign secured lots of rides as almost everyone who passed us wanted to have a chat with the travelling lads from Australia.

Because we always wore thongs, it was a little disconcerting when hitching at night, and we always walked down the white center line on the highway to avoid snakes. The snakes would lay on the road to suck up whatever heat was still there from the day. We were particularly concerned about Puff Adders as they are back-fanged, and if you trod on one of them, they'd throw their head back and give you a nasty bite.

I also took a train to Johannesburg in 1971 with a South African friend from Durban. He took his motor scooter on the train with us so we could get around Johannesburg easily. He was visiting some friends in Hillcrest, a hippie hangout back then. We'd been there for about a week when my friend decided to stay for a while, so I hit the road to hitchhike back to Durban. I made it to an area called Underpants Creek, about 60 miles south of Johannesburg in the Orange Free State. The area was given that name because, in the Boer war, the Afrikaners had surprised the British troops in the creek bed and forced them to strip off to their underpants. The Afrikaners took the uniforms of the English soldiers and left them to freeze during the cold weather at night.

On the other side of the highway, there was an army training camp. It's not a good place to be for a long-haired surfer-type wearing pink cord jeans with all those crew-cut Afrikaner soldiers not too far away. I'd been waiting for quite a while for a car to come by, so I started walking to get away from the area. It got freezing out there at night, and it was starting to get dark. All I had were my jeans, a T-shirt, and my thongs. I walked a little way and found myself in a dip on the highway. Then I heard a car approaching from behind me and instantly stuck out my thumb. A gray Porsche 911 came roaring down into the dip and then blasted up the other side. Oh no! The first car I'd seen for ages, and it passed me by! Then I heard the car brake suddenly. And then the car came backward down the hill and pulled up beside me. The young man driving was about 30 years of age, an Afrikaner named Coos, as it turned out. Coos asked me where I was heading, and I said, "Durban." Coos said hop in. He had all the latest music on 8-track cartridges – Janis Joplin's *Pearl*, Joe Cocker's *Mad Dogs and Englishmen*, Rolling Stone's *Sticky Fingers,* and about 8 more cassettes of the best music stuffed in his glove box. As we hit the road again, he asked me what I'd like to hear.

I selected Janis Joplin's album *Pearl* and placed it into the tape deck. This was heaven! A nice warm car and the best music to listen to. Then, instant panic! How far was Coos going? To the next town?

With trepidation, I asked him how far he was going. He said he was going to Durban to hook up with his wife, who was holidaying there. I couldn't believe it! Coos said his wife was staying at the 5-star Malibu Hotel, which is less than 100 meters from the 2-star Dolphin Hotel where I was living! As usual, my luck held out, and once again, I was saved. After some of the things we discussed as we were driving to Durban, I kept my word on the surfing lessons and gave Coos a couple of classes. He was super keen but had so much more to learn. But living in Johannesburg would have made it difficult to learn how to surf.

Speaking of hitchhiking, when Paso and I were heading to Cape Town and were in the Garden of Eden - well over two-thirds of the way to Cape Town – a car finally approached. We stuck out our sign but then noticed it was a two-door Mini Minor Coupe. We dropped our thumbs and waved a 'hi.' They gave us a wave and disappeared down the road. We turned around to face any oncoming "traffic," of which we had seen very little that morning. Then we heard the screech of brakes. We turned around, and the car was stopped in the middle of the road. The two passengers exited the car and ran toward us. We couldn't figure out what was going on. The two guys were staring backward and forward as they ran. Paso and I were puzzled. Suddenly, a herd of elephants emerged from the bush on the right-hand side of the road and trampled over the car, squashing it into the road. The elephants carried on, trampling in the distance. We were all shocked by the event. Wow! Welcome to Africa!

Now, it seems, another two hitchhikers were joining us on the road.

Clayton's Birthday

In the photo above, the woman at the right is my godmother's daughter, Sandy Moore. Sandy was born a month before me. When her mother was filling out my birth certificate, she mistakenly put Sandy's birth date as my birthday: 2 June 1949. I was actually born on the 6 of July, 1949.

All of my parents, friends and relatives were stoked when Mum gave birth to me. When mum was 19, she was badly burnt when burning rubbish. Her nightdress caught fire. Mum spent 18 months in hospital recovering from the burns she received. She spent her 21st birthday in hospital. The doctors said that she'd never have babies. But then she proved them all wrong and had me, and then 3 years later, my sister was born.

Over the years, this incorrect birth certificate has proved to be a nightmare. It wasn't a problem at first; I just wanted to go overseas as quickly as I could and never bothered to change it. But before I went back to South Africa in the mid-2000s, I decided to have the birth certificate altered back to my actual birth date. But by then, of course, due to the nanny state, you couldn't use a copy of the birth certificate; you had to produce the original. The hospital where I was born in Ashfield burnt down in the fifties, along with my original birth certificate. So, I emailed my passport back to the passport office with a letter explaining what had happened and to have it changed to my correct birth date. It was obviously too hard for the bureaucrats, and it sat in a drawer until I realised that I was about to fly out and asked for it to be sent back. This they did. Just in time! So now my birthday is "Clayton's" birthday, and I have to remember that whenever I deal with anything government or health-related, I have to use my Clayton birth date.

(When's a beer, not a beer? To quote actor Jack Thompson: "If it's not a full-strength beer, then it's a Clayton's beer.") As I said about the dates on my passport - it's a fucking nightmare!

Fear of Flying

I've always had a fear of flying. It's because I'm not operating the aeroplane. I have to trust the crew to know what they are doing. The only really scary flight I had was when Christine, me and our two-year-old baby Tush were flying home from Adelaide in 1982 after a visit to her parents and her brothers and sisters. What should have been an hour-and-a-half flight turned into a 22-hour nightmare.

Just after take-off, when the wheels were being stored under the wings, there was this hideous screeching sound, and when the wheels came to their final resting place, a loud bang was heard, and the plane shook dramatically. It was quite scary, and all of the passengers were spooked by the sound. We continued flying until the captain addressed us on the intercom. He said there were a few difficulties with the landing gear and that we would now be landing in Canberra.

When we landed, the pilot brought the aircraft in on the right-hand wheels. They weren't sure whether the left-hand wheels could take the impact of landing. Everyone leaned to the left when the plane dipped over to the right. Even the frequent fliers had the look of fear etched onto their faces.

We somehow made it, and when the left side wheels touched down, everyone breathed a sigh of relief. Once the plane had stopped, we looked out the window, and there was the ground crew standing beside the left-hand wheels. The ground crew were amazed that the plane had landed safely. The captain came back on the intercom and said we could wait for the next plane to Sydney or we could catch the buses they were providing. The captain asked us to put our hands up if we wanted to wait for the buses. Virtually everyone put their hands up. So after a wait for the buses and then the long bus ride back to Sydney airport we eventually scored a taxi for the last leg of the trip home.

And to top things off, the taxi driver was a bit of a driving maniac. He scared me a few times more than the flight to Canberra! At long last, we made it back home again and were so relieved to have survived the experience.

The Lockdown Blues

In early 2021, during the Covid-19 pandemic - one of the biggest scams ever committed on the Australian public - I figured I'd spend some of the $1500 given to me every fortnight by the government to not go to work and stay at home.

Due to the authorities' constant misinformation and blatant lies, I composed a song called The Lockdown Blues, performed by Snakebite Slim (me in disguise wearing a Russian gas mask.) With only two simple guitar chords and my untrained singing voice, I took the living piss out of the NSW and Victorian police forces with their fascist approach to protesters of the lockdowns and the uselessness of the Covid-19 "vaccine" - along with ridiculing the politicians and the so-called "health experts" involved with the fiasco.

I placed the music video on Rumble because Facebook would have immediately banned it.

I emailed my family and friends the link to the video as a laugh. Around 90 or so people saw it on Rumble. But then Vera sent the link to a friend of hers in Moscow who owned his own radio and television station, along with a popular blog that was viewed by thousands of subscribers worldwide. To my surprise, the video went viral, and I became a worldwide "musical" star.

A joke made for my family and friends went supernova! I couldn't believe it and we all had a huge laugh over the outcome.

Alison

When I was 18 years of age, I went to a party in West Pymble with my girlfriend, Alison Price. Alison lived one street away from the party. The party was held at up-and-coming film star Jacki Weaver's house. She was living with her parents, who were away for the weekend. Jacki was 18 at the time, too.

I was so keen to meet Jacki that I walked straight into a full-size glass window beside the front door. I didn't even notice it! There was broken glass everywhere - and I walked straight through it!

I came out with a few scratches, minor cuts and bruises. Jacki and Alison were really concerned, but they calmed down when they saw I wasn't hurt. No hospital is needed. Then Jacki noticed all the broken glass on the floor. This pissed her off because the window would have to be replaced before her mum and dad got home. She gave me the cold shoulder at the party and Alison and I left soon after.

I can't blame her.

But my entrance certainly livened up the party!

Tereza

Brennan and I have been hassling Tereza to move out of the house she was living in and visit Australia for the first time since 1977. She was always hesitant about selling the house in South Africa. Maybe because it was once her mum and dad's house, it was where she grew up. She knew the neighborhood. Well, she did at some point in the past. But now the area has changed so much. It's now almost full of Muslims, and the area is becoming unsafe for anyone white. Tereza gets on well with the Muslims, but the area is just not safe anymore.

This was proved when her housemate Stephen was killed in late 2023. This shocking death made Tereza think clearer about what she could do in the long run.

Stephen was at the house and opened the front gates to put the car away when some African robbers attacked him in the driveway. He died of the wounds he received during the attack.

That's South Africa. There's no stopping the violence. It happens every day all over the country.

Sadly, Tereza has led a sad life in many ways. His partner Aubrey, one of South Africa's most respected architects, died when he committed suicide in the garage at their home. He was addicted to Class A drugs and couldn't kick the habit no matter how hard he tried. So, in the end, he took his own life. He gassed himself in the car. Tereza was so shocked when she found him that she damaged both her hands trying to break the glass window to get into the car. But sadly, he was gone. It was too late.

I went to visit Tereza in 1995. I helped her get over the incident as best as I could while I was there. Having her once husband with her did make it more comforting I suppose.

On a lighter note, when Brennan was 15, he was with a group of friends, and they decided to graffiti the concrete walls surrounding some of the houses in a nearby neighbourhood. The cops caught them spray painting and took them into custody. After being questioned, Brennan reluctantly told the police his mother's number. The police called Tereza and told her what had happened.

She asked the police to 'Teach them a lesson. Drive them around for a while, then bring them home.'

The cops agreed and took off with the three helpless kids in the back of the paddy van. The spare tyre - which was usually secured - was loose and rolling around, bumping into the kid's legs. They tried to control the movement of the tyre - but occasionally, it would bump them hard.

Lesson learned! Well done, Tereza.

When I was visiting Tereza and Brennan in 1995, I was with

Brennan one day at the markets at the far western end of Durban. I noticed a witch doctor's stand and went over to have a look. I was staring closely at the bottles on display. In one of the bottles, I slowly recognised what I was looking at was a human heart! I went and told Brennan and we noticed the witch doctor glaring the evil eye at us. We retreated and, jumped in the car and took off. I looked out the rear window and he was giving us the eye, big time! Then Brennan said there had been lots of reports in the papers and on the news about witch doctors using Muti medicine. Muti has elements of human parts. It's supposed to help with the magic.

So that's why all the news reports were saying there were now 14 missing teenage Indian girls! Bloody hell!

Out of my four blood kids, I'd have to say that Brennan was the most like me. He has the same body language and he always lands on his feet when things go wrong, as I seemed to do.

In 2024, Tereza came for a visit and stayed with Brennan, his wife Sarah, and Tereza's (and my) two grandkids, Cade and Alexa. She stayed for a month at Brennan's. Brennan's step-sister Lindel was coming out from the UK for the last two weeks of Tereza's visit here. Lindel was a respected artist based in London. Tereza helped Brennan complete some painting around his new house and started talking about selling the house in South Africa and moving out here.

So, hopefully, it will happen.

Tereza is a good friend of Vera's, and I spoke with her on the phone while she was here.

A Tale of Two Cities

Well, one city and two tales. To be precise.

Sydney and the difference in lifestyles.

Victor had a hard time when he moved out of home. He had six dogs. All of them are huge. He had no luck getting properties. He couldn't live with us. We moved from the house on Taiyul Road into a unit.

He'd been working on getting a place in Public Housing and now has a small unit in the Twin Towers at Redfern/Waterloo. He can now concentrate on the documentary series that he's putting together. It's already launched, and now he's observing the results, as per click per view.

It's about *"People who like Dogs."* And he's trying to build that brand and get a decent following.

We looked at the views of Victor's best long-form video and the best short-form video.

I've made short video blogs for the school's website and they were all less than a minute. 58 to 59 seconds maximum. They were getting good views.

So, we made some plans to get the production moving forward by attracting an audience with short-form videos. If people only have a short amount of time to watch a video, then make sure it hits them hard with a couple of usable pointers. So, we'll see how the approach works.

But speaking about the two different locations, comparing Narrabeen to where Victor lives is truly educational when it comes to the different lifestyles we're living in.

At Narrabeen, everything is clean and tidy. The people are reasonably friendly. Yeah, there's always a little bit of rubbish lying here and there, but nothing to get alarmed about.

Your cars are always safe, whether on the property or on the street.

Where Victor's living now in a two-bedroom apartment with six big dogs is a tight fit. There's rubbish lying around outside, and the cops come around often. Once, they found a set of legs sticking out of the garbage disposal system at the other block of units. The disposal ate the top half of the body, but couldn't digest the rest of it. No one was ever charged over the death.

There's a kids' park near the units, but kids hardly ever use the park because of the needles lying around.

But the view from the balcony is pretty awesome. He's on the eighth floor. Both buildings go as high as twenty-seven stories! *The Twin Towers.*

I always go for a walk with Victor. Everyone appears to

know Victor because of his dogs. The indigenous people all talk to him but ignore outsiders.

We also played in the sun in the park for a while. These young Indigenous women were playing basketball and were really good at it.

The people relaxing in the park were cool. There were some friendly indigenous people and some friendly white people as well.

When walking down the street to the shops, I noticed a cop on the footpath standing outside an all-night store. There was another cop in a parked police car texting on his phone only a meter from the policeman on the sidewalk. The cop on the footpath was friendly. He seemed a little stoned.

When I asked Victor what the cop was doing, he said: 'Just keeping the riff-raff away.' And for sure, there was plenty of riff-raff around the place.

When walking back to the building, we saw rats running across the ground in the car park area. The dogs chased them, and the rats ran under the cars and then dived up into the engine compartment to get away from the dogs.

Bloody rats! And the cockroaches running around in the car park added to the story.

When upstairs, the view from the balcony allows you to see

most of everything going on at street level, plus an outstanding 180-degree view of the area and the distant hills.

Down in the street, there are Indigenous people playing music and dancing along to it – mixed with everything else going on down there. People go outside to the car park to smoke a cigarette. Shows consideration. Well done.

The people living here are poor. And in some cases, desperate. But they had a sense of stoicism about them. They banded together. They hung out and swapped stories of their lives or of other people's lives.

I noticed that when smoking cigarettes, the locals in the area smoked them all the way to the butt and then dumped the butts on the ground.

On the Northern Beaches, you'd see half-smoked cigarettes lying about the place. You could literally see the difference between the rich and the poor in these two suburbs just by observing people's smoking habits! With enough money on the north side of the harbour, people were not concerned about throwing half a cigarette away.

It's interesting how small things like that could give you so much information about the two different suburbs Victor and I were living in.

Now, here's something really frightening. (If the legs in the rubbish disposal weren't enough!)

There was a man living across the corridor from Victor's unit. He would come knocking on Victor's door every day, asking for three cigarettes. It was always just 'three cigarettes.'

Who knows? As Victor said: "There's a lot of crazies living here."

When Victor's neighbour didn't show up for two days, Victor knocked on his door repeatedly and got no answer. So he went downstairs to the security guard section and told the security guard he was worried about his neighbour. The security guard said to ring the police. Victor responded, 'You're the security guard. It's up to you to call them.'

Two weeks later. Nothing had happened. And Victor and his other neighbours could smell something nasty seeping into the corridor from the man's flat.

One of them called the police. The poor police who had to deal with a decomposing body. The police can be really tough when they have to be. The "three cigarettes a day" neighbour was a big guy. A huge guy, in fact. Later Victor said he'd heard that the man was on Meth. But to be as huge as that, as a Meth head, you'd expect them to be wasted, dissipated. But, as I said, this man was *BIG*.

How's that for the Housing Commission, eh? Two weeks after reporting a suspected body to security, nothing was done about it. No one at the Housing Commission seems to care.

But, hey, on the brighter side, Victor also had a thing going with the dogs.

He had a Seagull Patrol business using Honey, his lead dog, and the other dogs. The dogs would all be on leashes. But Honey was mounted on an electric skateboard, and when a bird appeared down the walkway, Victor would send Honey down on the skateboard and scare the seagulls away.

Victor and the dogs attracted a large crowd of onlookers. The people loved the dogs. And the pay was good, too!

Staying at Bianca's

It was great staying at Bianca's when I ventured north.

I remember when I was teaching Bianca in 1999 and later Tianjin in 2003 how to drive, I used Ingleside as the best place to teach a beginner. We could drive through the back streets of Ingleside, then out onto Mona Vale road, the main road, then turn left at the lights to Ingleside, and do the whole course again. There was hardly any traffic and a safe place to learn the much needed skills required on our deadly and crowded roads.

One time, when Bianca was learning, she ran over a green snake on the road. It freaked her out, but when we did the loop and came back, there was no snake on the road. Bianca, to say the least, was highly relieved.

I spent time at Bianca's in 2023 with Tianjin and her kids. Ben (Tianjin's husband) and Vera were both working. Then, later, in early 2024, I came back up with Bianca. She had driven with Denali and River to Sydney as Denali had a booking with a doctor. I came along for the ride back to Byron when she was finished. After a short holiday, Nick and Bianca bought me an airline ticket back to Sydney. At the end of my holiday, I spent the final night with Brennan and his family. Brennan drove me to the airport the following morning for my early flight home.

When staying at Bianca's, I always slept in the outside office. It was a good setup. I had my laptop online, and there was a double bed in the other half of the office. Tianjin and the kids slept inside the house.

Tush slept in the office, too when he was staying at Bianca's. As Tush noted, the stars at night were just amazing. There were so many of them! You could clearly see the Milky Way. There are hardly any lights in the area at night. So, all of the heavens were visible.

Bianca and Nick's house was a nice place to stay. The grandkids, Denali and River, were awesome to play with. And there were so many interesting things nearby to explore. Plus, Brennan and Sarah lived on The Gold Coast, out the back of Burleigh Heads, with two more grandkids to play with.

It's always a special time when I know I'm heading north. It's a special place up there in the far north of NSW.

Wrap Up

All of my kids have done acting classes with me. The classes have helped them achieve the goals they are chasing in their lives. Brennan is now a senior video editor and director with a company based in the ACT and works from home on the Gold Coast. Victor does a bit of acting work every now and again, and Bianca and Tianjin run their own company, *Lawless Foods* and Tianjin is also a yoga teacher. Ksenia is starting her own company, *Global Opulence Collective,* after working for years in the corporate world. Tush has sold his house and is moving to Adelaide for a while.

And now, I'm teaching one of my grandkids, 9-year-old Zuela.

It doesn't get any better than that! ... Mum and Dad would be proud.

I have four blood kids and two step kids, along with seven grandkids, who I love with all of my heart. But it's not always smooth sailing. I've had problems with my kids. Some of them are my fault. But we've always worked it out in the end.

The picture above with me and my grandkids, taken in April 2023 - left to right: Denali, Cade, Zuela, Alexa, Rainer, River and Bowden.

I've lived for three score years and ten. Plus, five. At the age of 75, I hope I can add another 15 years to my life. By then, my grandchildren would be aged between 18 and 28 years of age.

I can then see for myself how they have developed as people. That's something to look forward to at the age of 90.

As Keith Richards said: 'The only problem with growing old is that you want it to continue.'

This memoir is part of my lifetime journey - from what I can remember anyway!

I hope you enjoy it. Because I certainly did!